Tooth and Claw

TO LUCY +
      ANNABELLE,

MANY THANKS FOR
   YOUR SUPPORT,

   YOUR PAL,

Terry Mitchman

Terry Mitchum

Tooth and Claw

Olympia Publishers
London

www.olympiapublishers.com
OLYMPIA PAPERBACK EDITION

A CIP catalogue record for this title is
available from the British Library.

ISBN: 978-1-80074-519-3

This is a work of fiction.
Names, characters, places and incidents originate from the writer's
imagination. Any resemblance to actual persons, living or dead, is
purely coincidental.

First Published in 2023

Olympia Publishers
Tallis House
2 Tallis Street
London
EC4Y 0AB
Printed in Great Britain

Dedication

In memory of Simon Wood.
You were, and always will be, my friend.

Acknowledgements

Special thanks to my friend, Eamonn, for initial proofreading, encouragement, and bouncing ideas.

Author's Foreword

I don't remember the exact date, but I remember the exact circumstances behind the creation of Rex Llewellyn. I and a few friends (all rather geeky) had sat down one night in the summer of 2017 at my friend Alix's house to play the Pathfinder role-playing game. I was playing a human barbarian. At some point during the evening, Alix put some YouTube videos on. It was just a few music videos, by a fairly obscure French band I'd never heard of, to break up the long, though still very enjoyable evening.

The band was Caravan Palace. The second video to come on was Lone Digger. It blew me away.

It was, admittedly, one of the most shocking music videos I'd seen in years, and I don't shock easily. Anthropomorphic animals (cats and dogs, naturally) ripping each other to bloody bits in a neon-lit strip club, set to an edgy yet bouncy electro-swing tune. It was dark, it was stylish, it was moody, and for the life of me, I could never remember what our adventuring party achieved that night, but I'll be damned if I didn't remember every note of that song and every speck of blood that almost gushed out of the screen! It just wouldn't leave. It's still in my head now.

Cut to a couple of months later. I'm walking the mile or so to the job I had at that time: telesales for a double-glazing company. Not the most stimulating of jobs, to be sure, but it put beer money in my pocket. On this walk, an idea struck me: why not expand on Lone Digger? A detective story told from the other side of the events? It was quickly forgotten in the dull drudgery of the job, but it stayed filed away somewhere in my mind.

Cut to March of the following year, and I'm once again unemployed while the rest of the world had seemed to move on around me. And also, to my dismay, without me. I felt weirdly isolated and depressed. Then I remembered that idea I'd had more than half a year prior, and I started to write. And I continued, and wrote more and more, and other ideas started flooding in. The little shock I'd experienced soon turned into a nuclear reactor of creativity.

Though Caravan Palace and Lone Digger were the starting point (and still form the nucleus of this book), they certainly weren't the end. I had accidentally created a world I wanted to flesh out and explore, that same stylish and gritty world of the video, but fully realized, as seen through the eyes of an overweight, hard-bitten Pembrokeshire Corgi detective who's been through enough bullshit to last a lifetime. It was a weird mishmash of the furry subculture, electro-swing music, real-life animal behavior, film noir tropes, classic Looney Tunes, and a society that was a bizarre cultural and technological hodge-podge of Raymond Chandler's 1940s and a filthier, more morally bankrupt version of the modern world.

So, in a way, you could probably call this Lone Digger fanfiction. In the end, all I have to say is this: thanks to Alix, Zac, and Jim for that one night of Pathfinder so long ago, and thanks to that one French electro-swing band that I'd never heard of (but still continue to listen to) for turning up all the beams.

Terry Mitchum, 2018

I wake up in my office, yesterday's paper crumpling off my face. There's a knocking at my door. I turn my bleary eyes to the worn-out old clock on the wall opposite my desk. Three forty-five, it reads. Dammit all. It's past noon, and my landlord is calling for me. I hate that ass, and I'm not wrong in calling him that. He's a mule: mother was a horse, father was a donkey. Being a cross-breed isn't exactly a stigma any more. That's the way things are around here, especially in this day and age. Unfortunately, his ever-so-loving parents didn't clip him when he came of age. He thinks he's the Saints' gift to women, even though all mules are sterile. It makes for some rather awkward living conditions when your landlord is banging someone upstairs because he really can't keep it in his pants. Anyway, he's been riding my hump worse than a camel lately to pay my rent, and today's payday. I almost gag at the smell of the pomade he puts through his bristly mane as he sidles his way in, greasy as a Tinseltown predator looking for his next conquest.

"Got the cash for me?" He says in that sleazy, Lothario voice of his. Haven't had many clients recently, to be honest, so I'm walking a razor's edge as far as money goes. No murders, no thefts, no missing animals for me to track. I'm a private investigator, if you couldn't tell already. What you definitely couldn't tell is that I'm a dog. Not ugly, an actual dog: my dad was a dog and a cop, his dad was a dog and a cop. It's in our blood, I guess, like a manifest destiny.

Where are my manners? The name's Rex Llewellyn. I'm a Corgi, a down on his luck private investigator, and in serious danger of going broke. Seriously. If you'll allow me to enlighten you on the finer points of our breed, I will. Us Corgis have had a long line of tracking, hunting, and upholding the law, all the way back to… I don't know when, at least as far back as Llanfargoch. That's across the Atalantic, somewhere in the Isles. I'm proud to be a dog in myself, but if I can be totally candid, I'm ashamed of the way most dog breeds are going these days. Every one of us is loyal to a fault, but that loyalty is turning inward of late. Most dogs these days are loyal to their own and nobody else. Kind of explains the gang culture that's grown up around us, certain breeds especially, and don't get me started on those 'dog supremacist' nutjobs. It's kind of like inbred thinking.

Cats are bad too. I don't know why, but every high-paying job in this city is held by a cat. They're the yuppy rich kid types, think they own the world, parading around like supermodels, preening and purring. I'm not bigoted or anything, but you've got to give history its dues, what with chasing them up trees and such. The language barrier was the spark that set the whole cat and dog thing on fire.

Anyway, my landlord has called me out, so I slip the ass a couple of bills. It's enough to keep him happy, but I guess I didn't really need to eat properly for the next few weeks, anyway. It's at this point, a few minutes after Eduardo leaves that she walks in. A zebra. Exotic for my tastes, but a client is a client, as long as her money's good. She seems kinda flustered. Eduardo must have made a clumsy pass at her on the way up, probably tried to slap her ass to be a big burro, like he tends to do, but I turn on what little charm and professionalism I can muster and offer her a seat. We sit in the usual places, me behind my desk, her on the other side, out in the open with no close walls behind her. The feeling of isolation can set into more flighty animals if there are no barriers or other members of their herd present, but she sticks it out admirably. She's decked out in brilliant greens, reds, oranges and yellows, her mane wrapped up in a turban, a throwback to her ancestral homelands. It might seem gaudy on any other animal, but compared to the black and white skin of a zebra, you give it a pass. In fact, it can look downright beautiful. She pushes a faded photo towards me over the desktop, shifting aside discarded bottle caps, crumpled papers, long-dead cigarette butts, and past-it biscuit crumbs. She's in the frame, much younger than now, and beside her is another zebra, just a tiny slip of a thing. There are tears in my new client's eyes as she asks me the question. And it's the one question I've been waiting for all month.

"Can you find my little sister?" she asks.

It's just six words, but in that one instant, I find myself inexplicably invested. I don't know what it is about this zebra, but there's something I can't ignore. Maybe I'm better than I give myself credit for, an old sentimentalist with a kind streak? Maybe it's her affluent appearance, all decked out in her native colors, that flashes big, green dollar signs in my droopy, weary eyes? I dunno. Either way, I keep an open mind on the situation at hand. It's only natural for a gumshoe. Her emotions seem sincere, but I know from being on the force that sincerity can be fleeting. I name the fee for a search-and-catch (as I like to call them), and she's more than happy to put some money up-front, a good couple of hundred. That should keep Eduardo happy for a while and pay for a few cigarettes and forties on the way, alongside a good meal or two, as long as my better nature doesn't dictate otherwise. I take her contact details, jotting them down in my notebook in case anything turns up (her name's Ziva), and I ask her what she can tell me about her sister.

Ziva tells me that her sister's name is Ayani, and that she'd disappeared from home a couple of months ago without so much as an explanation. There was no indication of what might have happened; no suicide note, no ransom demand, nothing. When the police couldn't turn up anything solid (not even a carcass on the freeway), Ziva had turned to the Yellow Pages and looked up any private investigators she could find. My name came up. I guess paying the few dollars a month for ad-space in the phonebook is paying off. It's better than being word-of-mouth, I guess. I ask if her sister had any enemies or any reasons for running away. She answers in the negative, and I know I've got my work cut out for me, with little to work from other than a faded photograph and biased character references. I tactfully leave off the questions when she starts dabbing her eyes and sobbing again, and I accept the case. I hate it when dames cry. I scribble my details on a scrap of paper from my notebook and hand it to her, just in case she forgets. Kind of like a receipt, if you will.

A few minutes after Ziva leaves, no longer gushing the tears, I'm on my way out the door. Can't let the iron go cold. Zebras are pretty rare in this city. They tend to stick together. Old ancestral memories and that kind of shit, dodging the old cheetah prides that long since died out. Then again, there are plenty of the zebra creed around here, mainly sick of their tribal ways and looking for a better life, somewhere that the pattern of their skin can raise a buck. And yeah, a buck is a dollar, though the bucks that come down for fun on their daddy's money aren't the most pleasant folk to be around. Gore you as soon as look at you. Monarchs of the Glen are the worst for at least two reasons; the attitude and the antlers.

Anyway, I start by listing the places that expatriate zebras might be. Dive bars, strip clubs, any place that a zebra might be noticed. Oldsburg has a multispecies demographic, but even then, there are rarities. Trust me, there are a lot of places that an attractive-looking zebra can turn a quick dollar, and given what I know of Ziva and the photograph she showed me, her sister is likely to turn a few heads.

I keep away from the lowest areas, where any sort of exotic animal could make a low living turning tricks. Most of us can't breed like that, so it's easy and pretty safe money, though the odd outbreak of inter-species STDs isn't unheard of, and trust me, they can get nasty sometimes. I keep to the places that might be worthwhile for a runaway. Something in my dander tells me that this zebra girl isn't so hard on her luck that she'd stoop so low as to sell her body, not with the way her sister seemed to hold herself and the amount of green she was willing to throw down. A few calls to my sources later and I find it. It's a strip club just out of sight of the regular populace, down in Coldwater, the cheapest side of town. It took some deductive reasoning to figure out that Ayani would most probably not want to be found, and Coldwater is the neighborhood to do that. It had a shady reputation in my grandpa's time, and that reputation seems to thrive even now. I make my way out there, walking the many blocks into the rundown slum of Coldwater, and it doesn't take long for me to find the place I'm looking for.

This particular joint is called the Watering Hole. Strangely poetic, I think to myself, on more than one level. There's a big neon sign out front of a gazelle spinning around a dancer's pole; inviting for all the horny, male elements of society. Not really my thing at the moment. In fairness, it would have probably tempted me inside had I been ten years younger and twice as dumb. It's titillating, to be sure, if that's what you want. Still, business is business, and I've got some serious business to conduct.

It looks pretty much like any other strip club from the outside. The cop cars out front tell a different story altogether. Nobody stops me as I casually push open the doors, more concerned with shooing vagrants and keeping the local populace at bay. The long, dark entrance hall to the club is eerily quiet and smells like sheer terror. Several animals must have come through here in a hurry, and recently, trying to get away from something awful. I can tell something rotten is up, but nothing prepares me for the main room.

Inside is a massacre. Blood everywhere. The walls, ceiling, floor, everything; it's all spattered in blood. The neons around the bar are off, and several tubes have been smashed, spilling their powdery guts onto the floor beneath them. I flash my license to the first responder and take a look around. He doesn't argue.

The chalk outlines of several bodies have already been drawn amidst the chaos, wherever the pooling blood allows. The CSIs have put their little yellow evidence cones and police tape in odd spots, and the pigs on duty (and yes, they are actual pigs) tell me there had been a fight the previous night, and a nasty one at that. It turned ugly when a dog tried to be funny, to impress his buddies. Apparently, he tripped the waitress. She was carrying a round of milk shots to a bunch of cat frat boys, and because their drinks got spilled, they got mean. From the few statements the boys in blue had gathered, the dogs and cats had been glowering at each other all night. The waitress was a zebra…

This little tidbit piques my interest. This might be who I'm looking for. I can smell the musk of fear in the air and the fresh gore in my nostrils from the half-dozen or so patches of blood that are rapidly crusting on the dance floor, and I know I've got to work fast. The problem is that I'm an unknown quantity, just some bum who walked in off the street, as far as everyone else knows. Sure, I've got a license as a PI, and a reputation among the police, especially since I used to be one of their own, but I still need to tread carefully. However, a few smooth words to the officer in charge, not to mention doing a little name-dropping, and I'm back in the game.

The manager of the club is not exactly friendly, a very surly and rattled stag with a Skyelands accent and not enough points to be considered a Monarch. Given the shock that he's had lately, and the deer species' whole 'headlights' issue, it is understandable that he'd be reluctant to divulge any sort of detail. This is something that needs to be done, though, or else I won't eat, not that he needs to know that. Not to make myself sound callous, of course; Ayani's safety is of paramount importance to me, but I'd learned long ago that you look out for number one first, or you're no use to anyone.

I push harder in my interrogation of the big bastard, but not too hard, trying to appeal to his need to get the business back up and running. I'm surprised he even talked to me to begin with. When you interview deer, whether stag or doe, it's a delicate balancing act. Too soft and they clam up completely, expecting you to forget about the whole thing and go away; too hard, and they'll flee the situation — mentally, physically, or both. I'd been around this particular mulberry bush far too many times when I was on the force, so I know how to leverage it just right. Yeah, Mr. Stag tries his hardest to keep the information from me, all the bravado and that nonsense, snorting and frothing at the mouth, but eventually, he cracks, his antlers obviously bigger than his balls.

He tells me the same story as the pigs: a brawl broke out and there were several casualties, and a few mortalities, though I can tell he's downplaying it. That explains the blood all over the place, but he tells me more. Seems the guys on duty for the PD weren't as experienced as I was about gleaning co-operation. There'd been a mix of species at the club the previous night: dogs and cats, obviously, but also a few unusual folks. There'd been a couple of crocs propping up the main stage and throwing cash at the night's entertainment (Amber was her name according to the owner. A gazelle. She hasn't been seen following the incident, either), a fox and a swan sitting together, a sad-looking donkey that had been nursing a beer all night, the ox bouncer, and a bunch of snake boys, cobras, he said.

The snakes hadn't started the fight, but they were more than happy wading in, and I'm not surprised by that. Those bastards are worse than the way dogs are going. Call me biased if you like, but I speak from experience. Those slimy bastards are always trying some angle, usually for the worse. I'm sure of it. I've seen a whole bunch of them in my time, all types, patterns, and colours, venom or no. A smile from any one of them still creeps me the hell out, like they're planning something five moves ahead of you, even though you can't even figure out the game. And they're not afraid to kill. In this case, it was the bouncer who bought it from them, but not before ripping his killer's fragile lower jaw off and letting him bleed out.

Anyway, from what I've been told and what I can gather

by sniffing around as surreptitiously as I can (yes, literally sniffing around), this had been a deadly brawl. Snakes, cats, dogs, the bouncer, most of the clientele in a knock-down, drag-out fight. It was a powder keg ready to explode with a single spark, the tensions built up over the course of a couple of hours, the wrong animals in the wrong place at the wrong time. I can smell the blood, fear, and anger all around me. It's still palpable in the air, scenting or not, just this feeling of unbridled aggression. I take another breath around the floor and draw a few conclusions, though not many.

One of the dogs was first to die. His scent is the oldest. Then a cat. It gets messy after that, like there was a huge flurry of action that was over in seconds. The dogs are — or, should I say, *were* — Dobermans: attack dogs, the gangland heavies, mainly because the breed has no compunctions about their actions. They're usually the enforcers of whichever Pack-boss they work for. The packs have their dewclaws in so many criminal enterprises that a lot of their guys feel untouchable. Probably why that asshole thought it'd be funny to piss off some cats. Anyway, all dogs have a scent that's specific to their breed, so it isn't hard to pick up on the distinctive Doberman smell, though there's a heavy pall of cigar smoke around it.

Three dogs, three cats. The snakes are difficult to track, blood notwithstanding, because they don't give off much of a musk, but I estimate two to five of them. The croc scent is faint, but it's there; two, maybe three of them, though it's clouded by some rather repellent body sprays that they must have been wearing.

The fox and swan had sat in the same booth, not getting involved, as the manager had told me, over on the far right of the main floor, their scents mixed with the dry martinis they'd been slugging down. Dangerous for the swan, if you ask me.

The donkey is clear as a bell, smelly as all sin, and he'd been drinking a pretty awful brand of beer, probably the cheapest on the menu. A dockworker by trade, if the sea-salt undertone is anything to go by. I make a note of it in my book. The ox blood is pretty prevalent, too, mixed with the tang of something foul, possibly venom from a snake bite. The stage, with its central pole, just stinks of gazelle sweat and peach-scented body oil, and something oddly pleasant I can't put my finger on. In fact, the pleasant smell is everywhere, like a maddening undercurrent that I can't escape.

Still, I'm having trouble finding the scent of a zebra, or any other unaccounted-for equine. The owner, the pigs at the scene, everyone has told me a zebra was working here last night, but where is she? The hunch won't leave me. My dander is up, and I can't tell why. Something about this setup feels right and yet wrong at the same time. According to the statements I've picked up, she has to have been here. The nagging thought at the back of my mind and still tingling in my nose is near-enough definitive proof of that. Seems like the old sniffer has failed me, though. Funny, given that I'd closed cases with it before. Happens here that a dog's scenting ability can totally overturn a case, given only a little evidence as backup. More than a few high-profile cases are cut and dried based on scent. Why not here and now, though? What is it that feels off?

I check my watch as I leave the club. It's setting in for late evening, and I wonder where the time has gone (as I often do when I'm really involved in a case). The night has grown long, and I make my way back to my home.

* * *

Eduardo is having another one of his damn parties when I get back. I could hear the music from down the street; it's that loud. Double standards, if you ask me. He hosts shindigs that shake the very foundations of that rotted-out old shell of a building so that nobody gets a lick of peace, and we all have to put up with it. Anybody else makes the slightest noise, and he comes down on them like a ton of bricks, especially if he's in one of his more ornery moods, like when he hasn't gotten any in a few days. He hasn't followed up on any of his eviction threats, to my knowledge, but it's probably best not to antagonize the landlord, no matter how much of a jerk he can be. And he is a jerk of the highest order, but I'm not going to be the one to tell him that, not when he can change the locks on my door.

Speaking of which, I fumble in my pocket for my keys on the way up the metal steps to my office-cum-abode, a virtually rusted-out set of steps that should have been replaced decades ago, probably before Eduardo even had this building. Every step clanks like a lead weight on a stone floor. Then I suddenly realize the lights are off in my apartment. I know for a fact that I keep them on at all times if only to tout for business, or at least look busy. My hackles stand on end. Someone's in there. I flex the stubby claws on my right hand, and grip the little stun-gun I keep in my left coat pocket with the other (never leave home without it, if you're expecting trouble). Something *really* isn't right. My hackles cause a tingle in my neck. I sniff to make sure of any intruders, but the night winds have blown away any lingering scent of whoever might be inside, at least from out here. Damn. No signs of forced entry, but the door is unlocked. I grit my teeth, steel myself, turn the knob, and open it slowly.

As I click the light on, my hallway is the same as ever; the same old take-out menus, Sainted pamphlets, and stained runner rug with its frayed edges on bare boards, but that doesn't mean anything. The weak bulb flickers fitfully overhead, still warming up to the electricity. It's then that I smell something strange; an unfamiliar smell, grazer... No, she went away hours ago. Definitely couldn't be my client. I move as quietly as I can, given my ungainly frame, until I reach the door to my office. It's dark in there, and I'm not prepared for anyone with a gun, so I press myself against the wall just by the frame and give an ultimatum. Given my experience, that'll either put them at ease, make them bolt for the rusty old fire escape at the window, or force them out of hiding to find me. In the third case, it might give me enough time to get in their face and zap 'em before they can fire. Or I'll die. Three out of four isn't terrible odds. What the Hell, go for it.

"I know you're in there," I yell. "I don't have anything you want. Come out and we'll talk. Otherwise, I call the cops, and you're going down!"

I hear a small squeak from the corner of the office. Definitely not a predator. A predator would have either come raging out of the shadows with their wounded pride, or else waited silently for me to approach, deadly in the darkness. Can't be a robber, either. A burglar would have made an immediate break for the fire escape, or at least kept their mouth shut and tried to overpower me before going out the front door. The smell of peach wafts through to me, and I think I know what I'm dealing with.

I flick the light switch and turn the corner to find a gazelle sitting there in my office, off to one side, trying to cower behind a mound of empty liquor bottles and fast-food wrappers. *I really need to clean this place up*, I think to myself. I guess that this must be Amber, the dancer from the club. She's dressed in a tight black top and a denim miniskirt that hugs her muscular thighs, bred for jumping and running like her ancestors. The light, cropped denim jacket she's wearing is probably more to look good than keep out the cold. Everything about her accentuates her figure, from the tip of her horns to her breasts, to her curvaceous hips, to her cloven toes. Not exactly the kind of thing I'd expected of somebody that has essentially broken into my home. I pocket the stun-gun that I haven't realized until now that I've been gripping for dear life, pull my claws back in, and stumble through the mass of dirty clothes, assorted trash, and at-least-month-old papers to the gazelle.

She's really whimpering by the time I get to her, and she turns her face to me, her lips curled into a terrified frown. A single look into those tear-streaked eyes tells me more than I need to know. She's afraid. She's alone. She's weak and vulnerable and hates it. She's seen things... I crouch down by her and reach to her with a comforting hand, a gesture of sympathy. She flinches and shies away instinctively, covering her face again. It's understandable under the circumstances. She curls further up into a ball, shivering and shuddering like her skeleton wants to burst out of its skin. I quickly take my hand back and briefly ponder my options. I can see her quivering, smell the fear on her. She is absolutely terrified, more than anyone should ever be. I relax and let the loveable dog part of me take over from the hunter. You know, that one part with the big, sad, soulful eyes?

"Who are you?" I ask, in a soothing tone, already knowing the answer. This manages to get a flutter of attention from her exposed ear, and I can feel the tension dropping, like somebody has finally turned the heat on, the cold giving way to warmth. Her eyes turn to me, and there's a sense of trust that we dogs know about. She's still really shaken, her mascara forming black streams on the fine fur on her cheeks, but she composes herself enough to answer, faltering almost immediately.

"Uh... I'm... uh..."

Her whole body is once again wracked with tremors, the tension palpable. I know I'm losing her right then. Gazelles are flighty animals, even worse than deer. In the presence of any kind of authority figure, even just a strong personality, they generally run or go to pieces. I sit back off my haunches, letting myself fall gently onto the floor, just to establish a connection. I'm on the same level as her, on those bare boards. My relaxed posture and non-threatening ways have some pay-off.

"You must be Amber, right?" I ask. She nods shakily. "What brings you here?" I continue.

"I was dancing at the Watering Hole last night," she replies. "I was told you could help."

"I might," I say guardedly. "Depends on what you've got to tell that I haven't heard already. I want you to tell me the whole story. Your words, strictly confidential."

She looks at me wearily with those soft, brown eyes, and starts her story:

"It was kinda quiet," she began. "Jock was on bar..."

"The stag?" I ask, presuming it was the guy I talked to,

24

"Yeah," she replies. "He does that sometimes. It's not really his thing, being the manager and all, but he helps out when we're short-handed. Anyway, I remember there were two crocodiles at the main stage. They didn't cause trouble, just kept throwing money on stage, so I kept dancing. There were three Dobermans at a side-table, too. Tough-looking guys in suits with big cigars. Then these three cats came in. They were wearing letterman jackets; college boys, I think. They sat across from the dogs. Ayani was serving them milk…"

I know that milk has an effect on cats. Cow's milk, specifically. It's cheap as all hell, but the more they drink of the stuff, the more boisterous they become, sometimes violently. Since it's only them and hedgehogs that are affected by the stuff, there have been no laws passed against it. No point penalizing the many because of the few. But Amber's naming of the animal serving it really grabs me.

"Wait a minute," I interrupt, and pause for a moment, gathering my thoughts and formulating my words, "She a zebra?"

"Yes… How did you know?" Amber asks, momentarily stunned.

"She's who I'm looking for," I say. "Please continue."

"Uh… yeah. She was serving that night," she says, hesitating for just a beat before continuing. "I wasn't paying too much attention. The cats were eyeing the dogs; I know that much. I turned around during my dance. I was looking at the back wall… The music was loud, I could barely hear, but I kept dancing anyway. Then something happened. Something fast. I slid my hands down to my butt, and I felt something… hot… and sticky. I thought it might be my body oil running. The spotlights get warm, and it can run… so it made sense at the time. The music kept playing. Then I moved my hands up to my tits and… looked… my hands were covered in blood… so much blood. Then I turned around and…"

Amber pauses, wringing a tissue between her hands like she's trying to strangle it, tears welling up in her big, soft eyes again. I sit there, stoically, producing the pack of cigarettes from my jacket pocket and opening the flap at the top. She dabs at her eyes with the thoroughly throttled tissue, what little mascara she has left finally being mopped up, staining the tissue a horrible, oily grey color. I hate it when dames cry. Her voice dies in her throat, but I need answers.

"I need to know what you saw," I say, firmly but not harshly. "Anything you can tell me might make a difference. What did you see?"

She stifles a little sob and clears her throat, taking a rattling breath to try to calm herself. A few seconds pass, wordlessly. The air itself feels like it's closing in around us, just as anxious to hear what she has to say as I am. Then she continues, every word sounding like she's tearing it out from somewhere deep down in her soul, little more than a whisper.

"Bodies… everywhere. All three of the Dobermans… the cats… all dead. There was a cobra with his jaw ripped off… Hank was bleeding out on the floor from his shoulder… it was turning black…"

Cobra venom, I think to myself, satisfied at my earlier conclusion. That's what I smelled on the bouncer, and I'm guessing Hank was his name. That bitter scent of death. Tough break. This still doesn't answer the questions I really need answering.

"Was anyone else there?" I probe, needing to know.

"I don't know," says the gazelle, turning her eyes

downward. "I think everyone else ran."

"What about Ayani?" I ask. "Did you see her anywhere?"

"No," she replies resolutely.

I sigh, partially relieved, dropping my head and taking a cigarette from the packet. At least that rules out her being killed at the scene. I put the cigarette between my lips and light up. I proffer the pack to the gazelle.

"Smoke?" I inquire. She gingerly takes a couple of cigarettes, tucking one into her bra strap for later and putting the other in her mouth. Kinda cheeky, but I let it slide. I light it for her, as any gentleman should. Huh… since when have I been a gentleman? The smoke seems to loosen the strain she's under, however, and I can see toned dancer's muscles starting to unwind. I'd offer her a drink, too, but I've been dry myself for a couple of days.

"I haven't seen Ayani since then," says Amber, now less tense, exhaling a huge cloud of smoke. "I guess she must have hidden somewhere when the fight broke out. Jock called the cops, and I guess you know the rest. I've already told them everything I know."

"I do know," I say, but there's still something niggling at the back of my mind. Or, more accurately, at the back of my nose.

"Tell me, did Ayani wear any particular fragrances?" I ask. "Strong perfumes, deodorants, anything like that?"

"She told me once that she sometimes wears dog pheromones," she says. "We get a lot of canine customers, so she puts a lot on. She says they tip her better if she smells like them. A lot of the girls do it. I just prefer body oil. It smells better to me."

That was one piece of the puzzle I needed right now. It

was no wonder I couldn't sniff out a zebra when she smelled like a generic dog! That was also probably what I could smell all around the club, that weird scent I couldn't put my finger on. I allow myself a tiny smile of satisfaction. Apart from the tragic events that had led up to that point, and though it's nowhere near complete, I have a slightly better picture of what might have happened to Ayani after the fight. I raise my head again and look at Amber, a strangely inquisitive smirk breaking over my face.

"Still doesn't tell me how you got into my office," I say, bemused.

"Your landlord let me in," she says. "I told him I was looking for you. And I turned all the lights off. You were wasting money."

That jackass Eduardo. A little tail comes his way, and he'll do anything for her. I don't know whether I should punch his lights out for letting a strange woman into my apartment without me knowing, or kiss him for accidentally delivering a material witness right into my lap. I stand up, my knees creaking from the strain, and help her up, teetering on her stiletto heels as she rises.

"You got a place to stay nearby?" I ask. "Family? Friends?"

"My mom lives in the Pastures," she says. "It's not far. I'll manage."

The Pastures isn't the best neighborhood, but it is pretty close by. At least with it being a mostly herbivore community, it doesn't have quite the same gang presence as other places in this city. I suppose the best way to describe it is 'poor, but honest'. Knowing what kinds of creeps can be out at night, though, I offer to call her a cab, and she agrees. I sit at my desk and pick up the phone, calling a local cab company that I tend to use when I've been at Sam's Bar & Grill for a few too many. She just sits there in the cracked, worn-out leather chair I usually reserve for interviewing clients, just across from me, silently puffing on the cigarette. Her hands are still giving off minute tremors. I book her a taxi; my buddy Sid is pretty surprised I'm reserving it for somebody else and that he's not going to Sam's to do it. Once I've hung up, it only takes about five minutes. In that short time, an awkward, stony silence pervades the room, mingling with the swirling clouds of smoke. A car horn sounds just outside, and I show Amber to the door. She descends the steps, her heels sounding a clattering counterpoint to the raucous music coming from Eduardo's pad. I close the door, considering my next move, what I've just learned swimming lazily through my head.

I'm idly munching on a dog biscuit in the dim light of my office, the cigarette smoke still hanging in the air like a host of phantoms. I look down over the dim pools of lamplight in the street just below my window, not entirely sure what I'm looking for in them. Dog biscuits are one of the more harmless of my many vices, though it's a vice that's done me no favors in the past. It's part of the reason I got retired from the force. I was getting too fat, and it started affecting my knees in a bad way. One physical later, and I was setting up for private work, but not before demanding a license from Commissioner Talbot. The old owl knew I'd been a good cop, so he saw no reason to deny me. The fees were a bastard, though. Bureaucracy and all that shit, though I'm still convinced it ended up lining Talbot's own pocket, whether he knows it or not.

Anyway, the thoughts of the past day start to form in my mind, and I consult my case notes. A missing zebra working as a waitress in a strip club, with an affluent-seeming older sister, if the amount of money she's paying me is any indicator. I don't work cheap. Family squabble, maybe? I slump down into my chair. *Maybe it's time to call in a few favors,* I think. There'd probably be somebody at the old precinct that could tell me a few more details, maybe see if this Ayani character has any kind of record that would lead me in any kind of direction. It's not like I can use any old Gamewell phone without a valid badge number. Maybe she's been in some serious trouble and had to leave her family? It's possible. I also quickly scribble down the dog pheromone clue. It might be useful in the future, especially if I come across that scent again.

Then there's the brawl at the club, with at least eight fatalities. I could easily put that down to inter-species tension: cats and dogs very rarely get along amicably. However, there is something tugging at the single thread of doubt in the back of my mind. Call it a hunch, but something about the whole set-up was off somehow. The Dobermans that had been at the club were obviously with the packs, made men with suits and cigars, at least from what Amber had told me. Though it's not inconceivable they'd be in a dive like the Watering Hole, it certainly seems out of character. Somehow, I figured they'd be into the more upmarket areas, like the Blue Aces Casino or the Velvet Dream, up in Northside across the Holbrook. They wouldn't be seen dead on the cheaper end of the spectrum in Coldwater. I mean, sure, they have a lot of business interests in the district, legal or not, but it still strikes me as unusual. Either way, they wound up dead…

I slump further into my chair and tilt my head back to gaze

at the ceiling, with its cracks and yellowing paint from too many years of nicotine, the biscuit jutting out from between my teeth like a cigar. I suddenly realize how tired I feel. I fold my hands on my lap, and I feel my eyes begin to close.

I smell blood. Poison, seeping, blackening. Hissing cats and barking dogs, teeth and claws flashing against the neons. Big, soft, brown eyes. A gunshot, and Boscoe hitting the floor amidst smoke and dust. Black and white and black again, and a scent of home. Pain, and joy, and memory, and terror, clashing against the cliffs of nothing and everything all at once. Yellow eyes, like death itself, gleaming, hypnotizing. The violent crescendo of a swing band.

Time slows. The blackness closes in, broken by the sinuous shapes of cigarette smoke, brief and intangible in the streetlights. I start to drown.

I wake with a start, wondering when I'd fallen asleep, or if I'd even slept properly at all. The biscuit is now soggy in my mouth and crumbling to pieces, but I eat it anyway, if only to try and rid myself of the strange grogginess that comes with waking up suddenly. A little gentle activity, such as eating, will do that for a body. I could just as easily have fallen back to sleep, but something tells me that wasn't going to happen, just from taking in my surroundings. There is an almost eerie quiet around me until I really listen, and hear the low, distant thrum of traffic beyond my window. Eduardo must have called it a night at some point; there's no music from upstairs. Weak, grey light is pouring in between the blinds, and I figure it must be pretty early on a thoroughly cloudy morning.

I get up, brushing a few crumbs from my shirt and jacket,

and go to get my overcoat and hat. The morning looks chilly, and I need to get the last remaining cobwebs out of my head. A walk would do me some good, maybe as far as the convenience store and back again. I need to get a paper anyway, and more smokes. Unlocking and opening the door, I'm greeted with a blast of air that's something akin to a refrigerator. I know spring is on the way, but does it still have to be so damn cold?

Anyway, it seems a good course of action today would be seeing a few of my old buddies at the precinct, but how much help they'll be is another matter. If Ayani does have a police record, it'd probably be out of the question to ask for it in detail. I guess it depends on who I get to ask. McReedy would probably be willing to let it slide, or Mendoza, but I'd have better luck chewing through a steel girder than getting the info from Houlihan or Bose.

Before I know it, unaware that my feet had even brought me there, I've arrived at the store, one of those little businesses on a street corner that you feel comfortable visiting, if only from familiarity. Walking in, I check the headlines of the different papers that are splayed across the stand. Mostly politics, with a few bits of celebrity gossip thrown in, usually from Tinseltown. I disregard all that and settle for a copy of the Oldsburg Herald, the city's local paper, as I always do, and head for the counter. A few pleasantries with the duck behind the counter (I think he's the... son? Grandson? Nephew? He's related to the duck who I usually see, anyway), and I've got my paper, my smokes, and a bottle of whiskey in a brown paper bag stuffed into my pockets. Impulsive, I know, but I'm cutting down. Mostly. Anyway, it had been one of those nights.

I head back to my office and give the station a call. I've

already drunk a few slugs of the whiskey before I get an answer, the warm feeling creeping up my spine, dispelling the spring chill, and I'm idly flicking through the sports section of the paper. The Bluesocks losing to the Giants again. Luckily for me, it's old Henderson that answers. He's a good one, too; an aged Jack Russel desk sergeant that I go way back with. Hell, my guess is he must have been there before I was even born, but I don't let on about that to the old codger. Ever. I'm actually surprised he wasn't retired years ago. Then again, a good, honest, hard-working desk sergeant is worth his weight in gold, maybe even platinum.

"Ninth Precinct, Sergeant Henderson speaking," he says, his usual gruff tone.

"Hey Tony," I say with practiced ease and quiet relief, along with a subtle hint of familiarity. The edge on his voice softens.

"Ah, Rex, good to hear from you," he says, his voice displaying a hint of joy. "How've you been, my boy?"

"About as good as ever," I reply. "Listen, I need a favor. I'm on a case, want to do a little more digging."

"What about?" Says Henderson, his tone shifting defensively. He's had calls like this from me before.

"I need to find out about a certain zebra, name of Ayani. Don't know the last name. Possible criminal record, though I can't be sure," I say, choosing my words carefully, and giving away no more than I need to. There's a brief pause on the other end of the phone, and I sip at the glass slowly, licking my lips pensively.

"I'll see what I can pull up," says Tony. "But believe me, buddy-boy, you owe me. Records don't just find themselves!"

"There's a steak dinner and a few beers in it for you," I

say to him, knowing how much he loves his steak. "You're a pal, Tony. I'll be at the station around noon."

I hang up and pour myself more bourbon. I must admit, it's virtually the same lecture Tony gives me every time I call (which I don't make a habit of, by the way). I appreciate his concern, not just for himself but for his pups and grandpups. The least I can do is show him his time and effort is rewarded. That's not just as a former colleague, but as a friend.

I look through the paper for anything about the fight at the club. It's tucked away somewhere in the middle pages, and after a quick scan of the details, among the lurid, journalese language, it doesn't really teach me anything new. I should know better than trust the crime writers at the Herald for anything. They're more interested in moving papers than actually reporting the news, so only the highest notoriety crimes and the goriest of killings ever get more than a short column at best, and even then, it's overblown and sensationalized. In other words, details and accurate information are not their strong points. I guess that's why I usually skip over everything and check the sports section first, before skipping to the funny pages. At least they've got *some* journalistic integrity there, especially when it comes to baseball. Newspaper aside, I'd get some better answers down at the precinct, then maybe go pay Mr. Stag another visit later on.

I'm feeling a little light-headed by the time I get to the Ninth Precinct station, on the corner of Razorback Avenue and Longhorn Street in the Arbor Hill neighborhood, just the other side of the river. The sky above me is the color of a bruised eye. Probably drank more than I should, but I'm not slurring or weaving, so who cares? There's a cold wind blowing, and the fur on the back of my neck prickles in response. Feels like rain is coming. The typical scent of the Oldsburg streets is somehow muted today, not as dusty and oily as it usually is, but that could just be the booze dulling my nose. I'd given old Henderson enough time to pull up something surreptitiously, either from the police database or the physical files, so I make my way up the stone steps, past the recumbent lion statues, and through the heavy oak doors with their brass fittings.

In an instant, I feel like I've just come home. The gentle murmur of cops going about their business, the ringing phones, the rustling of files, the scent of stale cigarette smoke, coffee, and the occupants of the drunk tank mingling in the air around me. It feels real and alive, like an animal unto itself. The animal of the Law. It's funny how people associate different animals with the law. An ass's stubbornness and inflexibility, a bull's strength of body and of purpose, all that jazz. I never bought into that way of thinking. To me, the Law is its own animal, tame but also wild, a creature of order amidst a world of chaos, but that still does what has to be done.

Anyway, I remember the corridors of this station house like the back of my paw, and one scent in particular: Henderson's pipe tobacco, Wild South Extra Mature. One wrong sniff of the stuff to a sensitive and unprepared nose feels like it could stun a horse, but Henderson always swore by that brand. Might even be why he's always been stuck as a desk sergeant; his nose probably tapped out. Anywhere you go in this station, there's always a faint undercurrent of his trademark smokiness. I could probably navigate these offices blindfolded by just picking up on that smell. It's like a direct link to the old terrier himself, so that's what I do. It'd be easier than tracking him down by asking around. I hand-wave the officer at reception, a young crane with his beak stuck in a comic book, and he doesn't even notice me waltz right past him, or probably doesn't care. He's too caught up in the adventures of the Coyote Kid or Doc Solomon.

The trail leads me past the interrogation rooms with their sound baffles and two-way mirrors. Those rooms have always put a shudder in me, ever since I was a cadet. It was an open secret among the officers what went on in some of those cubicles, out of earshot, out of sight, and most definitely out of mind. The beating of prisoners was almost like a pastime among some of the officers I'd served with, and Commissioner Talbot turned a blind eye every time. Commissioner Radcliffe pretty much encouraged it before the DA came down on him and tried to reform the force. Not like a lot of those scumbags didn't deserve it, but it did make me wonder just how guilty some of them really were, or how genuine their confessions. Public outcry was something that happened rarely. Seems the animal of the Law has a taste for blood, and a reputation for fear, like an apex predator.

I pass the bullpen, and it's busy as ever. The hubbub is loudest here, the smell of coffee, sweat, and cigarettes strong and pungent, those familiar cries of "no, ma'am" and "we'll be right on it" wafting up from the din. There's a mix of species in here, dogs and pigs mostly, sat at various typewriters and telephones, and I can't help but listen to some of the specific calls as I pass. They're mostly simple and petty matters, nuisance behavior or vandalism, maybe the occasional shoplifting, but there's a few I overhear about gang activity in the Hollows and Coldwater. Seems the packs are having trouble, I think to myself, not to mention the vigilance committees. It's then that I realize I can smell somebody else, just ahead of me, coming into scent range. Somebody I don't like at all. Marcus Tilton.

He's a mean asshole. Looking at the fat hog, you'd wonder how he could ever have made the cut at the academy. I'm pretty short, but I practically tower over the guy. On the other hand, he's about twice the weight I am, and a lot of it is pure muscle. He's a brute, but a charming and subservient brute towards the right authority. I'm kind of surprised to see him in an ill-fitting suit and trilby — complete with a tastelessly loud tie — rather than a uniform, but before I can turn and walk the other way, he's onto me.

"Ey, Llewellyn!" He grins, all too familiarly, clasping my hand and squeezing it like a nutcracker. "How've ya been, buddy? I heard you's retired."

"Yeah," I say back, through gritted teeth and a feigned grin, partly from the stink of his hair oil, partly from old animosity, and partly from the pain in my crushed paw. "Just dropped in to say hi to some old buddies."

"That's a shame, pal," he continues, oblivious to my obvious attempts to get away. "Guess those dog biscuits really did get to ya in the end!"

He belches out a huge laugh, snorting between breaths, his curved tusks a dull yellow. I quietly seethe. Ignorant swine. It's not that funny, especially since this had been the only career I'd ever known or wanted. At least he hasn't brought up...

"Oh, hey, did you hear?" says Tilton, his voice suddenly turning half-serious, much to my surprise. "The boys are gettin' together at Sam's on Sunday to remember Boscoe."

That name. My ears twitch, and the hackles start to rise on

the back of my neck. My jaw clenches tight, and a low growl starts in the bottom of my chest, drowned out by the commotion around us. Why, oh why did Tilton have to bring up Boscoe?

"We was wonderin' whether or not to invite ya," he continues, just as obnoxious as ever.

My hands have balled up into fists, one tighter than the other. If I slugged him, here and now, I'd probably get a few days in the joint for assaulting an officer, but it would be worth it to shut this bastard up, shut out the memories. Luckily for the fat swine, another voice interrupts what could have been a fine right hook from yours truly.

"While I live and breathe," comes a sultry, female voice. "Rex Llewellyn, back at the old Ninth. How've you been, Rexxie baby?"

I am stunned. My ears twitch and prick up. This is all I need. Tilton stops his little diatribe suddenly and takes off his hat sheepishly, only amplifying the foul stench of hair oil. I turn to where he's looking, and my stomach finally sinks out of me and into my shoes. It's her.

"Do you mind, Marcus?" she asks. "I'd like a little word with our mutual friend here. Go play somewhere else."

She arches a finely plucked eyebrow at Tilton, and he shuffles off in the manner he usually reserves for when he's been chastened, or when he's up for a disciplinary hearing. He'll probably take out his aggression on some poor sap later — prisoner or co-worker — but for now, he's left me with her.

Ah, Jennifer Cassidy. Five-foot ten, a hundred pounds soaking wet, and every bit of her spells out trouble, for me at least. She's a whippet, blonde, slender and graceful, with gorgeous, slanted eyes and fine features, hips that could kill and legs for miles, a figure emphasized by the white blouse, pencil skirt and high heels, all wrapped in a huge, imitation fur coat. She's the kind of dame to make any man fall head over heels, but she's never been the marrying type. Trust me, I know.

"Jenny," I say, smoothing out my tie and looking furtively at the parquet flooring. "It's... good to see you again."

She gives me one of her little smirks of amusement, the ones that she always gave to try and make me blush. She's up to something; I just know it.

"It's good to see you, too, honey," she says, sighing lightly. "Sorry for interrupting your little chat with dirty old Marc, but it looked like you were in need of rescue. He's a detective in Ad-Vice now, so he's been stomping around feeling important. At least, that's what they tell me."

I shuffle my feet restlessly, but I know she's right. Administrative Vice, huh? Certainly suits the guy.

"Thanks," I mutter before realizing something was strange about her being in the station. "Why are you here, Jen? I thought you were covering the gossip columns in Tinseltown."

"Oh, baby," she purrs, better than any cat I've met. "You know how to push a girl's buttons. I'm here for the same reasons you are. A missing animal that these numbskulls can't crack?"

Dammit, Jen. Following my leads. Jen moonlights as an amateur detective. Maybe Ziva had little faith in my ability as a snoop, so she looked to less reputable sources? Not that Jen is a bad investigator, but I'm still sore about it. It always seems that any lead I get, she also has her little claw on the pulse. If things had gone differently back then... I pull myself together and answer.

"Nah," I say, trying to be nonchalant. "You must be mistaken, babe. Just saying hi to a few pals."

"Oh?" says Jenny, savoring that one syllable like a candy treat. "From what I heard, there was a massive brawl down at the Watering Hole in Coldwater. Death and blood, you know how it is."

The blasé manner with which she gives that little quip makes my fur crawl. She has that overall effect on me whenever she discusses cases. She's a journalist first and foremost these days, so she lives in her own world of high-class parties and press conferences. She does some sleuthing on the side, but it's as though she sees the private detective business as some sort of game, a hobby to keep herself from getting bored. Still, it makes me realize that she has been following the same leads, and I need to be a step ahead.

"Yeah, nasty business," I say, brusquely. "Probably some gang rumble that turned ugly."

She stands there for a minute, shifting her hips left and right, probably trying to get more out of me. I'd fallen for her tricks before, but not another time. In the end, she gives in, knowing she can't get any more out of me.

"Take care, Rexxie-baby," she says, sauntering off from the bullpen, turning a few heads as she passes. "But this isn't over."

Dammit, Jen. As far as I know how to press her buttons, she definitely knows how to press mine. And she's pressing them in all the wrong ways.

My nose finally leads me to Henderson. He's sitting in his office, and he's more than happy to see me. I guess the duties of a desk sergeant don't really allow for a lot of social interaction. He greets me with that huge smile of his, the same one that makes you wonder if he is genuinely pleased to see you or just really thirsty, squinting happily through the thick lenses of his glasses.

"Rex!" he says, shaking my hand like a long-lost comrade. I make sure to proffer him the hand that wasn't being crushed by Tilton. "Come have a seat. Let's have a talk about that zebra of yours."

"Great, Tony," I say. "What is it? Pulled in?"

We sit at his desk, immaculately neat and tidy as always. One thing you can always say about Tony is that he really takes pride in his work. He places his cola-bottle glasses atop his head, between his scraggly ears, and quietly rubs his eyes before answering.

"Nothing," he says, anticlimactically, his tone shifting to disappointment. "We've got nothing on any zebras called Ayani. Either she's new on the streets, or she's particularly conscious about keeping her nose clean."

That statement hits me like a punch to the gut.

"That can't be it," I exclaim. "She's been away from her family for at least a couple of months! She must have done something! Picked up for vagrancy? Or shoplifting? Anything?"

"A couple of months don't mean jack, son," says Henderson bitterly. "You should know that by now. Heck, I practically taught you that your first year on the force."

"I know, Tony," I reply, disheartened. "It's just really important I find this girl. She could be in danger."

"If she was in danger, my boy, you should really leave that to the proper authorities; namely, the police," he says gruffly, setting his glasses back on his muzzle.

He's right, of course, but the police haven't been able to turn up hide or hair of Ayani since she disappeared. There's a moment of quiet between us before Tony speaks again.

"I'm sorry I couldn't be more help, Rex, I really am," he says, finally. "But I think you're on your own on this one."

Once again, just like with the report in today's paper, I feel like I'm hitting a brick wall. Not only that, but Jen is probably one step ahead of me, possibly even more than that. I stand, half-defeated, and head for the door. I thank my old buddy for his time, renewing my promise of that steak dinner, and make my way out of the station, doing my best to avoid Tilton, skirting around him by scent alone. I don't think I could stand another conversation with that pig, especially if it's about Boscoe.

Once I get outside, with the smoggy clouds glowering above me, the rush of city smells replaces the musty scent of the precinct. It's always unpleasant, but it's just the way a city should smell. Car exhaust, dust, the street food carts, the musk of countless species all pressed in together, sharing a little plot of land that can barely contain them all. Like the station, it feels real, but sometimes it's too real for comfort. I'd bet those college-boy cats went looking for something real, something to take a bite out of, and they found it. Or rather, it found them, and it bit back.

It's late in the afternoon when I get back to my office, turning slowly to evening. The Watering Hole won't be open yet, so I put a record on the turntable and zone out for a bit. There doesn't seem to be another soul in the building, so I risk turning the volume up a little. The soft, soothing sounds of jazz fill the air as I sit in the same threadbare swivel chair, pouring myself more liquor into the glass I had previously discarded on my desk, and munching on another biscuit. It's comforting being surrounded by the sound of horns, saxophones, and clarinets. I take a long, slow draught of liquor and hold up the glass to the light, the legs of whiskey trailing their way down the sides. Speaking of legs, I wonder quietly to myself if Amber made it to her mom's place all right. I damn well hope so.

I feel disappointed that Henderson couldn't turn up anything, but like he said, just because Ayani's a runaway doesn't mean she has a history. Still, I find it kind of suspect that she's working at a low-end strip club. The music builds to a miniature crescendo that drops dead before signaling the second movement of the tune. I sip at the glass again, the prickly warmth of the booze dancing along my tongue. I light up a cigarette, wondering what I could have missed in my investigation, even at this early stage. I check my few notes again and scribble down that the girl I'm looking for doesn't have a record. Something still doesn't feel right, though, and I can't tell what. My dander just won't quit. It's like I know what's happening, but don't know at the same time. Detective's instincts, huh?

The second movement of the album kicks in, more subtle and less lively, but still with that signature Earl Monkton swing. I rock back and forth on the chair absently, like a metronome to the music around me, trying to think of some connection that I'd missed. Ziva, my client, has cash to burn, at least from the figures she is willing to pay me. Ayani, my target, had run away for some reason. They are related, sisters. Something had to have happened between them, or maybe with someone they knew…

It's then that I hear the faint sound of a knock at my door. It must be Eduardo, I figure. Damn, I thought he was out. I haul my fat ass out of the chair, stumbling slightly. Got to lay off the booze for a while, I think. It won't do to interrogate someone later while half-soused. The knock comes again, more insistent than before.

"All right, Eduardo, for cryin' out loud!" I slur, stumbling through the debris across the floor. "No need to break it down!"

There's another knock. I check the chain is on and undo the lock.

"If it's about the music…" I begin, opening the door, but the words catch in my throat as I don't see the mule's leering face at the door. I'm momentarily confused before the clearing of a small throat draws my eyes downwards. There's a short raccoon standing on my doorstep, in a pretty snazzy-looking, charcoal-grey pinstripe suit and a pair of wire-framed glasses. My brow furrows for a moment, questioningly, before he says anything.

"Mr. Llewellyn?" he inquires in a vague Wilstonian accent.

"Who wants to know?" I answer, wishing I had my stunner on hand. There's something about this guy puts my teeth on edge. Must be the suit.

"I'm here on behalf of Mistress Onyelé," he says. "May I come in?"

Onyelé? I don't recall that name, and if I do, it's only a vague impression. He's business-like in his mannerisms, formality personified, though I don't unbolt the chain. I know better than to do that in this neighborhood, no matter how sharp the other guy's duds are. He notices my blank expression and takes the hint to continue.

"Mistress Ziva Onyelé?" he prompts, and it all falls into place. She never told me her surname — I don't usually ask it of clients, if only to distance myself — but now that the little guy mentions it, the name does have the sound of the Zebra Nation language. I ease up a little, but I'm still on my guard. I absent-mindedly sip from the glass, licking away the few drops of alcoholic dew that still cling to my whiskers before answering.

"You're from Ziva, huh?" I say, warily. "Can you prove it?"

He puts his tiny hand into his coat pocket and deftly flourishes a scrap of paper. It's the receipt I gave Ziva with my details on it. I'd recognize the cheap paper quality anywhere. I close the door, unbolt the chain, and open it up again fully.

"Okay, shorty, come on in," I say. He visibly winces at me calling his height into question, but he comes in anyway, his polished loafers clicking on the bare boards before being dulled by the old rug. Got to say, it's funny for me seeing a raccoon in a suit. Most of the raccoons I've ever met were the ones I was bundling into the back of a black-and-white, ready to be processed for vagrancy at the station. They're called trash-bandits in this town for a reason, but his accent is throwing me for a loop. Wilston is an ivy-league college town, a place of culture and education. And money.

"I apologize for the sudden intrusion, Mr. Llewellyn," he continues. "Mistress Ziva would have come herself, but she is otherwise... indisposed. At a function, before you ask."

I wasn't going to ask, but it's nice of him to offer that up. Kind of makes sense, too. I wouldn't be surprised if Ziva did attend a lot of 'functions', the amount of cash she seems to have. Lucky for some, I think, but I'd probably be bored stiff or paranoid beyond belief. A 'function', to me, is a bunch of stuffed shirts in tuxes talking hogwash about their stocks and bonds, swilling gallons of brandy from preposterously big glasses, smoking a factory's-worth of cigars until the ceiling lights are blotted out, and showing off their conspicuous consumerism while secretly shoving a knife in the other guy's back. Give me a gang rumble any day. At least with that, you *know* someone is out to get you.

"And you are?" I ask,

"You may call me Mr. Pettibone. I am on retainer to Mistress Ziva. That's all you need to know," he replies primly, adjusting his glasses slightly.

I don't think I'm going to be getting any more from the little guy about himself unless I dig for it, which I honestly could not care less about. Still doesn't answer the question as to why he's here, so I voice it.

"So, what's the deal?" I ask. "Why are you here? The case?"

"Indeed, sir," Pettibone says, curtly. "And your rather boorish handling of it."

I bristle at the word boorish, but I take a good slug from my glass, and the feeling subsides, my hackles cooling down. I take in a good breath, and yeah, Pettibone smells of equines, like he works closely with them. A servant of some sort, maybe? Still have to fight my corner, though.

"I do things my way," I say to him, trudging back to my desk and grabbing up the whiskey bottle. He turns silently to me, fastidiously avoiding the trash around him, cleaning the lenses of his glasses with a tiny silk cloth.

"It's a most… unorthodox way," the raccoon replies, as tactfully as he can manage. "And it may cause unwanted attention. You do realize what this could mean to Mistress Ziva."

"No, I don't," I tell him, straight-up, with a hint of booze-laden cockiness. "But let me guess: scandal? Loss of status? An honor-killing, maybe?" I slump back into my chair, a wry, sour smile on my face at that last remark, and pour out some more hooch from the bottle, the pale, golden liquid cascading gracefully in the dim light. He stiffens visibly, putting the spectacles back on his muzzle.

"Nothing that far," he says, a sharp edge to the comment, and irritation building in his voice. "But a lady of Mistress Onyelé's standing and influence is certain to be adversely affected by any errors in judgment you might make. Her father has a position to maintain…"

My ears prick up as Pettibone catches himself before he can spill anything else, the glass in my hand halfway to my lips. So Ziva and Ayani do come from a wealthy and influential family after all. That kind of background can certainly help the case.

"Position?" I inquire slyly. "What position?"

"I am not at liberty to say, sir. I have already said enough," he says, somewhat beaten. "I can merely ask that you conduct yourself in a more discreet manner. We have been informed that you made inquiries at the Ninth Precinct this afternoon regarding certain records."

Damn it. Someone found out about Henderson's little escapades on my behalf. Probably Bose, that creep. He'd sell his own mother if there were any trace of profit to be made in the transaction. I'd expect no less from a hyena, in all fairness.

I sigh deeply and put the glass down, its weight clinking slightly on the desk. I guess I really have to play ball with this guy.

"So, in other words, keep this on the quiet is what you're saying?" I ask.

"Exactly," says the raccoon. "Or, regrettably, Mistress Ziva will be forced to terminate your employment." He pushes the glasses up his muzzle, the wire frames strangely gilding the natural domino mask of his fur. I consider my words carefully before I answer.

"Like I said, I do things my way, pal," I say. "But I'll try not to tread on too many toes. Deal?"

"That would be preferable, yes," Pettibone says, a dryness to his tone. "I suppose beggars can't be choosers. That is all." With our business concluded, I get up and lead him to the door. Before leaving, he turns to me, a serious look in his eye.

"Do not disappoint us, Mr. Llewellyn," he says. "We shall be in contact again."

The door clicks shut, and I listen as his tiny feet echo faintly down the steel steps. I strain to hear any other giveaway sounds, but if there are any, they're drowned out by the sounds of Earl Monkton and His Swingin' Seven emanating from the record player.

It's getting late. I'm walking the same cracked Oldsburg streets I grew up on, and I'm feeling grumpy. My feet are already aching, not to mention my creaking knees. I can drive, it's expected of a cop, but I can't exactly afford to run a car on the few paying clients I get, and the subway doesn't go where I need to be.

I'm halfway to Coldwater when the rain sets in. Just my

luck. Nothing but trouble at the station, then I get chewed out by a representative of my client for not being subtle enough, and now this. The day had started so nicely, too. *Yeah, right.* I allow myself a rueful little smile as I stop at the mouth of an alleyway under a streetlight, and fish around in my overcoat pocket for my smokes. Just hope the damn things aren't all wet.

A hand the size of and strength of a car-crusher grabs me by the elbow, and I snap around in shock, my hackles prickling up and my teeth bared. I'm in no mood for any more surprises right now. It's then that I see who grabbed me: an ox, over seven feet tall and built like a bulldozer, in a flannel shirt and worn jeans, his eyes dull, gleaming in the lamplight. He doesn't even register the barrage of rain on his thick skull and curved horns; he just stares down at me with those leaden eyes. I quickly lose the snarl. This guy looks like he could turn me into a bloody sludge with one of those anvil fists, then pound the sludge into mist with the other. Maybe it's best not to antagonize the goon. He speaks slowly, as oxen are wont to do.

"You, Mr. Loolin?" he asks, ponderously, barely able to pronounce my name,

"Er… yeah," I say, shaken by the fact that he knows who I am. Not like that hasn't happened today, but this guy legitimately intimidates me.

"I'm Bill," he intones. "Jock, tell me about you. He say you help."

Mr. Stag at the Watering Hole. How does he know this bruiser? And how does he think I can help? What is going *on* here? I try to speak, but the words catch in my throat. The dumb ox notices.

"Hank was my brother," he says, somberly. "He die."

As much as I was originally terrified of this Bill character, I allow myself to breathe again. He's the late bouncer's brother. Maybe he's got something I can use on the case, but I doubt it. It's more than likely that Jock pointed him in my direction, and the stupid creature thinks I can help bring his brother's killer to justice. Kind of impossible when the dogs in question are already bagged and tagged in the police morgue.

"Yeah," I reply. "Sad business. I'm sorry for your loss". You have to think slower and use smaller words when dealing with an ox. They're not very bright, though it's never a wise move to suggest that to their face because they can be as short on temper as they are on brains.

"Hank was a good brother," says Bill. "Jock say you help for Hank."

Oh no. It's just as I'd thought. This moron wants me to find the killer.

"Hank's killer is dead," I say, slowly and clearly. "I can't help with that."

"I know," Bill snorts, steam rising from his nostrils menacingly. "I not stupid."

"Oh," I say, taken aback and not wanting to get trampled by four-hundred pounds of ox. "Sorry, pal."

"Jock say to tell you things that might help," he says. "Hank know'd things. He tell me."

The rain isn't letting up, and I cast around for a shelter. I suggest a diner across the street, so we can talk somewhere dry. After nearly a full ten seconds of consideration, Bill agrees with me, lumbering along behind me. I could really use a cup of Joe right now, anyway.

I shake the rain from myself as we enter the diner, water

droplets splattering around me on the black and white tiled floor. It's an old dog trick, shaking yourself dry. Once the overpowering scent of moisture from my fur subsides, the equally overpowering scent of the diner hits me in the face like a truck. It's all there: the bitter tang of brewing coffee, the delicious smell of sizzling burgers, the three-year-old grease oozing from the busted extractor in the kitchen, the sickly chemical aroma of the urinal cakes in the bathroom. It's enough to make me want to hurl if I cared to do so, but I swallow that feeling and gesture for Bill to take a seat.

I sit at the cracked Formica counter, and Bill slumps heavily onto a stool beside me, though with how wide the guy is it feels like he might as well be sitting in my lap. The tall, gangly fruit-bat behind the counter asks us our orders, and I check my wallet. Only a few dollars left. I just order a cup of coffee, wanting to preserve what little cash I have on me. Bill, on the other hand, orders not just a coffee but a decent-sized stack of flapjacks with maple syrup. Guess it takes a lot of energy to heave that huge bulk around. Although the bat starts to object to Bill's request seeing as it isn't breakfast time, a single stare from the ox sends him scurrying off, with only a leathery rustling of his wings behind him. As soon as the bat leaves for the kitchen, I look around to see if anyone's listening before Bill and I can speak. A donkey sat at a side-booth behind us, well out of earshot, and a rabbit in a rumpled business suit at the other end of the counter, picking over a depressed-looking salad. Nothing to worry about. I prompt Bill to continue.

"Okay," Bill rumbles. "Uh… you wan' know what Hank say to me?"

"Yes, Bill," I reply, patiently. "That'd be grand."

"Hank said he seen those dogs before," he continues. "The ones I read about in the paper. They die, too."

Other than being surprised Bill could read at all, I guess he means the three Dobermans at the Watering Hole on the night in question. Sure, the Herald had reported on the fight, but they hadn't published any photos of the victims or given their names, just a vague description of species. Trying to pry information that vital out of the cops was like trying to find an honest politician. But what do the dogs have to do with the case? I only have a few seconds to think about this before Bill continues his story with all the implacable force of a glacier.

"Hank say they with the packs," the ox continues. "They brag about it to his face. Think he was dumb. Think they was big dogs, like alpha. Hank say they start coming to the club just over month ago."

The dots start to connect in my mind, and my ears prick up, but I have to quash the feeling of elation as our coffees arrive. The pack-boys started turning up at the Watering Hole just over a month ago. Ayani had disappeared two months ago. There has to be a correlation. Once the fruit-bat's back in the kitchen, I press on Bill for more.

"Did he say if they did anything strange?" I suggest, and Bill's brow knits in quiet thought.

"He say they looking at new girl. *A lot*," he says, the wheels in his head slowly clicking the words into place. "The zebra. Hank not like it."

That kind of makes sense to me. Ayani was known to wear synthetic dog pheromones to get bigger tips, but so did a lot of the girls, at least from what Amber told me. But it's the way Bill stresses the words 'a lot' that concerns me. It suggests more than the hard-wired reaction that's common in dogs

52

toward females, and that's a troubling thought. What had those bozos been planning?

"They ever cause trouble for this zebra?" I ask.

"No," says Bill. "Just drank and watched dancers. That's what Hank tell me."

I sip at the coffee, my lips curling at the fact that it's only lukewarm, not to mention gritty. I try and think for a second, but the thoughts don't come. The rabbit down the counter pushes his plate aside and gets up to leave, grabbing his briefcase and umbrella as he does. The sizzling from the kitchen in the back flares briefly before subsiding. The door flaps shut as the rabbit makes his exit. The bat brings out Bill's unusual order before sidling down the counter to collect what's left of the rabbit's meal. Bill sits quietly beside me, shoveling slabs of flapjack into that huge trap of a mouth, his teeth grinding noisily. I breathe in deeply to clear my head. Then it hits me. The faint whiff of sea salt coming from the booth behind us. My eyes widen imperceptibly as I recognize that smell. It was sat in the corner of the Watering Hole, nursing a crap brand of beer, on the night eight animals tore each other to shreds.

I snap to where the donkey was sitting, but he isn't there. No flushing from the bathroom, so he might not be in there, either. I feel Bill's eyes boring into the back of my neck, and I turn back to the ox, his face puzzled, not an unfamiliar expression for that species.

"What goes on, Mr. Loolin?" he asks, dribbling crumbs down his flannel shirt, but I barely register the question. My hackles are up. I give a half-hearted excuse to hit the bathroom, rushing in only to find the blank porcelain and aluminum faucets staring back at me. I wait a minute or two so as not to arouse suspicion, then I make my way back through the diner. I look where the donkey was sitting. Bill is once again stuffing his face with flapjack, ignoring my return. Something that looks like a driver's license or I.D. card is on the worn-out, faux-leather seat beside me. I casually lean down and scoop up the card as I pass, unnoticed by Bill or the fruit-bats in the kitchen, and stuff it into the pocket of my overcoat. I'll have to inspect it later.

"You was long time, Mr. Loolin," says Bill, the words muffled by the oats and syrup jamming up his teeth.

"Yeah," I reply nonchalantly. "Coffee goes right through me."

I've managed to shake Bill by the time I get to the Watering Hole, and the rain has slackened off some. I gave Bill a promise to remember his brother and do right by him. How could I not? It's not every day that an ox hands me a clue that could prove useful or maybe even vital. It certainly casts the confrontation in a different light.

Speaking of lights, the neons are back in full glare across the front of the Watering Hole, the gazelle dancer in the sign swinging jerkily around her pole. The pounding bass from inside the club virtually shakes the street beneath me, sending tiny shivers into the soles of my shoes, and into my feet. In Coldwater you don't let things stagnate or fester too long, or you're on the streets with the down-and-outs that infest the area like a plague. This neighborhood is like a polyp on your backside: unpleasant, uncomfortable, maybe painful at times, but unchecked, it could grow into a tumor. Luckily, that's never happened, but it's still a dangerous place to be after dark, especially if you're not native to the district or if you're flashing too much wealth around. There's no Johnny-on-the-Spots to be seen, and that puts me on edge. I knock on the big doors, and a little grille slides open. A puff of steam greets me that reeks of booze and foul breath, enough to make my stomach lurch sideways.

"You have membership?" says a rough, gravelly voice from beyond the door, a strange accent behind it,

"Rex Llewellyn," I reply. "I'm here to talk to your boss. I need to speak to Jock."

The grille closes, and there's a pause as the shmuck behind the door engages his tiny mind. I wait for what seems like an eternity before I get a response. My hearing tells me the guy hasn't budged an inch. Lazy bastard. The grille slides open.

"Sorry, no salesmen," he says before slamming the grille shut again. Rude, if you ask me. Also dumb. I wait a minute or two before knocking again. The grille opens, and the same blast of stinking air hits me.

"You have membership?" comes the voice in a more hostile tone. I take a good sniff of the air. Vodka, definitely that. Seems this guy's had a few too many already. Sloppy for a doorman.

"I told you, I'm here to see Jock," I say, somewhat louder than I need to. "Go get him! It's important business!"

I hear a grunt of frustration before the grille closes once more, and my dog-hearing picks up the heavy footsteps traveling along the massive corridor, even over the ruckus from within. I light up a cigarette and wait, the smoke forming ever-changing patterns against the glow of the neons and the harsh glare of the streetlights, punctuated by the occasional drop of rain that flashes through. I'm about halfway down my smoke when the unknown voice returns through the open grate.

"Jock says he see you now," grizzles the voice, and the huge doors open to me. I step through to be greeted by the sight of a huge bear with white fur stuffed into a white shirt and black waistcoat. Ruskie, I'd bet. It accounts for the accent and poor grasp of the Anglish language. The noise of the main room is louder here, but I can still hear my shoes clicking along the floor in their regular pattern. It's a sound that's, strangely, both comforting and ominous. Once I open the main doors, though, all bets are off.

I'm blasted with a tidal wave of noise and scents. Booze, bass, sweat, chatter, body oil, raucous laughter... I reel from the sensory overload. It's damn bright in here, to say the surroundings are so dimly lit. There's somebody up on stage, still wearing what little clothing she has left, a ferret, acrobatic in her movements, and loving every minute of attention she's getting. The customers of all species are throwing bills on the stage for her. Guess they think they'll get to see more fur if they pony up more dough.

I make my way to the bar, trying to keep myself from skidding along the slick floor. They probably waxed it after the CSI boys finished up their investigations, and anything spilled on it has likely made it even more slippery. The lighting is way too low to tell for sure, but it seems like they got the bloodstains out. There's a young filly behind the bar. She smells vaguely appealing, doused in the fake dog pheromones that I've grown accustomed to from my earlier sniffing. She's dyed her mane bright blue, and she's wearing a tight, baby-pink crop-top and black leather miniskirt, carefully worn to almost (but not quite) show off her goods, the dental floss of her undies poking up over her belt. I sit my ass on a barstool, and she smiles that fake smile that all servers have in their repertoire, the one reserved for the customers, especially if they're having a bad shift.

"What can I get you?" she asks, with strained politeness, just audible over the heavy beats from the main stage. I lean in to reply.

"Bourbon," I say, trying to be heard above the din. "Double. I need to talk to Jock."

She must have understood what I said, because she's tipping a nod and gesturing to another server, a chubby female raccoon in an outfit that's just as revealing but definitely not as flattering. The raccoon nods, and my server disappears through a door behind the bar, presumably leading to the manager's office. It's then I notice she hasn't even served me my drink. Just my luck again. At least I haven't paid for it yet. I'm dreading what it might come to, but I think I should be able to afford it, even with the few bucks I have left. Might have to make it the only one tonight.

I sit there at the bar for a few minutes, the ear-splitting cacophony of music and chatter behind me. I have to hand it to the DJ for knowing his audience and for keeping the music loud but at least tolerable to a dog. I reach into my pocket and pull out the plastic card I found at the diner, squinting at it through the smoky haze and flashing lights. Sure enough, it belongs to a donkey; Benjamin Orcowitz, age 38, male, five feet ten inches, one-hundred ninety pounds. Seems it's a license to operate heavy machinery if I know my vehicle codes. The plastic feels rough, like there's dirt caking on it, and it smells terrible, a combination of wet donkey and sea spray mixed with motor oil. I confirm my guess that he works at the docks, or at least handles things that come through there. Easttown, maybe. The Riverland Park wharves are another possibility, but more ocean-going traffic comes through the Easttown docks, and it's not as far from here.

I stuff the card into an inside pocket of my suit as the door behind the bar swings open, subdued lighting pouring out from it. The filly is leading, and Jock is following. He has to stoop slightly, his crown of antlers almost scraping the frame. I note the notches in the frame above his head, probably left there by him when he's been careless. He nods to me silently, a business-like look in his eyes. I notice and nod to him, and he turns back into the gloomy corridor behind the door. The filly slides a double bourbon into my paw before I can follow. She smiles an infernal grin.

"It's on the house," she mouths to me, a devilish glint in her eye. She probably knows how badly my presence is discomfiting her boss, and she's relishing it. I slug down the hooch in one swift, searing gulp and make my way behind the bar into darkness.

I'm shown into the manager's office by Jock, and he hurries out of the door, leaving me to contemplate. I have to say, his office is pretty nice. Apparently, pedaling titty pays. Oak paneling, deep-shag maroon carpets, huge desk with assorted executive novelties, tastefully erotic art on the walls, abstract sculptures on little mahogany tables, plush leather chairs, even a standing humidor cabinet full of cigar boxes. I'm examining one of the finer pictures, of a lady wolf reclining regally on a sofa, the titillating details artistically obscured by draped silk sheets, when Mr. Stag finally deigns to join me. By my guess, he's probably been berating the staff, judging by his cold demeanor and hunched shoulders.

"Gotta say, pal," I strike up. "You've got decent taste in paintings. Not one for the sculptures, though."

"Mah taste in art is none o' your business," he retorts, that thick Skyeland brogue clipping his syllables. "An' ah'm no' your pal. What is it ye want?"

"Just following a few leads," I say in an almost cryptic manner. "I've got a few questions about your girls, and about your customers lately. Or should I say, late customers?"

I see him visibly tense up, his ears twitching. I'm getting too close for this guy's comfort, so I should probably ease up on the wisecracks. I pull a cigarette from my pack. Last few remaining. Had I really smoked that many today? I guess I have. Anyway, I pop it into my mouth, unlit, and sit myself in one of those big leather chairs. I offer him the pack. Got to show some empathy, make some connection.

"Smoke?" I offer, hoping he won't take one,

"Ah'll have one of mah own, thanks," he says tersely, before sitting in another chair across from me and primly plucking a fat cigar from a wooden box by his elbow. I look to my own elbow, see that there's no box there, and mentally note that he's in control, the animal with the cigar. At least he thinks he is. We strike matches almost together, but I let him strike just a second before me to continue the illusion that he's dominant.

"Ah've told ye what ah know," he says, the acrid bloom of cigar smoke swirling amongst his antlers like a halo. "Why have ye bothered me again?"

"I've heard some interesting things from beyond the grave," I say, before taking a deep drag on my cigarette. "About a group of dogs that started coming around here a few weeks before the brawl. Dobermans."

The cigar sits uncomfortably in Jock's hand for a second before he taps out the ash into a marble ashtray. His posture shifts broodingly, and I know he's feeling the heat. I need to press that advantage before he gets too riled.

"Bill, your former bouncer's brother, told me that you told him I could help," I allow myself to lean back into the leather. "Seems Hank was smarter than you gave him credit for."

Mr. Stag shuffles a bit in his seat. He's nervous.

"Aye, I did," he concedes. "Only to get tha' big lummox away from mah bar. It's nothin' to do wi' me."

"Really?" I ask, an incredulous and slightly menacing tone in my voice. "His brother dies in your bar, protecting your ass, not to mention your staff and customers, and you say it has nothing to do with you? From what I hear, those suits had been hitting this place pretty regular for a few weeks. Got something to say about that?"

He stands from his leathery perch, the cigar drooping between his fingers, and he starts pacing. This is something I've seen only rarely. A stag with a brain and, I gather, something to hide. I turn on the soulful eyes shtick, that sympathetic dog look that I know so well, and he responds favorably.

"The packs have been pinchin' us hard of late," Jock says, a hard edge lining his words. "We're payin' a packet to 'em every month. Mah guess was they were here te put more pressure on, te get me te pay up more."

Protection racket. Old-school. Romantic. It's understandable that this guy didn't want to divulge it to anyone. The packs have lawyers that can slip their clients out of nearly any charge that they're not caught red-handed for, and the retribution would have been terrible if Jock had said anything to the cops or me. Not only that, but any business in Coldwater is a pretty easy target for the packs. I can sympathize with that. Still, it's not relevant to my investigation into Ayani's disappearance. There has to be something else.

"That's tough," I say to Jock. "But I think there's more to it than that. According to what I've heard, they'd taken an interest in one of your waitresses. A zebra, specifically. You know who I'm talking about, Jock?"

It's not a question, but rather a statement of fact. His ears prick up around his antlers, but he quickly regains his composure, sitting heavily in the chair at his desk and stubbing out the smoldering half of cigar in another ashtray, saving it for later. He folds his hands on the desk in front of himself.

"A'right," he says, dejected. "What is it ye want te know?"

"Names, Jock," I say frankly. "Details, credit card receipts, overheard conversations, anything that'd help."

Jock pauses and thinks for a few seconds before answering, a self-satisfied smile spreading over his face like he's beaten me. He sounds far too smug for my liking, too.

"Sorry, fella," he finally says. "Can't help you wi' that. They always paid in cash, and ah never heard any names mentioned."

"And your staff?" I ask,

"Tha's confidential," he says, just as smugly. "All legal, but confidential."

This is getting me nowhere. Maybe I should try another tactic. I rise from the plushness of the chair, my right knee grinding slightly from being sat for too long, and I cross to the desk, stubbing out my own cigarette in the ashtray alongside his remaining half of cigar. Jock waves away the small plume of dying smoke, and I smile coolly.

"I think you know plenty of folks who might have heard something," I say slyly. "So, what's a guy got to do to get a private dance around here?"

"Ya pay like everyone else in here. Why? No missus te go home te?" Jock says arrogantly before his brain catches up with him, and his eyes widen with the realization of what I'm suggesting. I simply grin wider, my fangs glinting in the subdued lighting.

I ask for the tubby raccoon on bar for my dance. It's not uncommon for dancers to work bar if the joint is short-handed, or vice versa, and given the last few days, there's probably more than a few staff staying home, shivering from fright. I feel both somewhat proud and ashamed of myself for having to strong-arm it out of Mr. Stag, but in the end, my reasoning brought him around to the idea, if only for the sake of his business. Two employees as material witnesses, one of whom is missing, possibly in danger, and a vicious pack of dogs baying for his blood if Jock rats them out publicly. And all I wanted in return for my help with this little incident was a dance. It was an offer Jock couldn't have refused if he wanted to.

I figure that dancers and staff would have a better chance than management to see and hear a lot of comings and goings, so I'm playing that angle discreetly. The raccoon leads me off to a dingy little side-room, away from the main stage. It's got a bead curtain and just enough red light to see by, but not enough to show everything clearly. The guard on duty — a badger, short, stocky and muscular — gives me a knowing nod and an unpleasant smile.

"Enjoy your dance, sir," he says, smirking over the words. The raccoon brushes him aside with ease, and we head into the gloom. It's quieter in here, the thrum of music from the main room still present, but only just audible. I dutifully sit on my hands on a worn leather sofa as she discards her shorts and top in preparation. She's wearing a bikini underneath, and it really doesn't compliment her figure.

"So, what's your name, honey?" I ask in a nonchalant manner.

"Ramona," she replies sweetly, as she closes the curtain to keep out prying eyes. I'd expected a Sapphire or a Crystal, or any other kind of stage name based on a mineral, but this girl doesn't seem the type to do that. She's got some underlying cunning about her, and, like I said before, she's heavier-set than the other dancers; less graceful, but pretty enough, and good at her job. Something is telling me this isn't her normal line of work, though. She doesn't have that dead-eyed look that a lot of exotic dancers develop over years of being leered over, and rather than business-like, her demeanor is downright friendly.

"Cute name," I say to her, and she giggles a little. "Been busy tonight?"

"Not really," she says, a little more conversational than I'd been expecting. "It's been quiet since that horrible fight the other day, y'know?"

"Yeah, I heard," I reply. "Nasty business."

Before I can say any more, the next tune has kicked in from the main stage. That's her signal to do her thing, and I realize I'm on a time limit. Once that song stops, I have to leave, so I've got to act quickly. Ramona starts swaying and gyrating to the music, no ballerina, but no clod either, running her surprisingly dainty hands through the thick, shaggy fur on her body.

"How long have you been working here?" I ask, still making small-talk to stall for time and hide my motives. I've got to skirt the issue without addressing it too directly, but I can't really afford to do that for too long.

"About six months," she says to me, absently, concentrating on her dance. "It's not what I want to do forever, but it's easy money, y'know?"

"Guess you must know a lot of what goes on here?" I suggest, trying to sound natural, but I can already sense it hasn't come across that way. She slows down her dance a beat, her back to me, her fingers toying with the string on the bikini top at the back of her neck. I hadn't noticed before, but she's pretty well endowed.

"I might," she says, peering over her shoulder, a hint of suspicion in her voice. "What's it to you?"

"Just interested," I lie, casually. "I'm a reporter for the Herald. It's for a piece I'm doing."

She spins around to me suddenly, quick as a flash, her eyes bright and full of life, twinkling through the gloom and the dark mask of her fur like two diamonds on a black silk pillow.

"Really?" she says, her excitement building. "That's so *cool*! What are you working on?"

She quickly plops herself on the sofa next to me, her dance totally forgotten, her bikini still in place. She's a little too close for comfort, and I can almost taste the floral perfume that hangs around her like a fog. Montrose No.7, I think? Talk about your unexpected fans, huh? Might as well keep up the pretense.

"Crime desk," I say, committing to the role. "I'm looking

into the fight that happened the other night. My chuckle-head editor let some wet-behind-the-ears cub reporter cover it, and they didn't do it justice. I'm looking for the truth."

I know this charade won't hold up under intense scrutiny, but she virtually squeals in response. Seems she wants her name in the paper or something. Sorry to disappoint, lady.

"What do you want to know?" she gabbles at me, excitedly. "I can tell you anything you'd wanna know, y'know?"

"Did you know the people involved?" I ask, fishing for clues.

"Oh, yeah," she says, her enthusiasm curbed suddenly. "Those poor cats. They were students at my university. That's U of O, by the way. Daniel Arden, Rodney Lynns, and Toby Sullivan. Pretty big on campus, y'know?"

So Ramona's a college girl. I can leverage that, if not on her, then on that scumbag Jock for possibly employing a minor as a stripper. Legal my foot! She's also given me the names of the cats involved. I make a mental note to look up the names Arden, Lynns and Sullivan. They might have connections to money, especially if they're attending the University of Oldsburg. Before I can say anything, Ramona continues her almost breathless profiling of the trio.

"They were on the basketball team together. I think they were pledge-brothers, too, with Alpha Tau? Poor guys. They really didn't deserve what happened to them, y'know? Our professors told us they'd died, and I knew three cats died in the fight, so I put two-and-two together. Mary Lansing, from Phi Kappa, she was totally heartbroken. That was Daniel's girlfriend, y'know? She cried for ages."

Smart kid. Before she can get any more out about her

college dramas, I quickly switch the subject, pulling my notebook from my pocket and jotting down what she'd just told me. This excites her more than I'd expected, clapping her dainty paws together. The lighting in here is shit, but I think I can scribble down what I need.

"What about the dogs they had the tussle with?" I ask. "Know anything about them?"

A puzzled look crosses Ramona's face, like she's trying to remember something. Then the lightbulb moment hits her.

"Yeah," she says. "Dobermans in suits? They'd been coming in pretty regular recently. Didn't like them. Too mean-looking, y'know?"

"Any mention of names?" I ask, trying to hurry the raccoon towards a conclusion before the music dies down and I have to leave.

"Yeah." She pauses. "I remember one of them calling another one Ziggy, and one of them being called Rocco. I think they called the other one... what was it... Paulie? At least, I think that's what they said. It gets pretty loud in there, y'know?"

Paulie is a new one on me, but the other two names I know by reputation and prior experience. Adolf "Ziggy" Ziegler and Heinz "Rocco" Rochmann. Those guys were button-men, ran with the Donati pack, and they were infamous for being the most unflinchingly violent sons-of-bitches in the whole organization: professional to a fault, unswerving in loyalty, but awful creatures nonetheless. I remember several times that they were almost brought in, but the pack's weasel lawyers always got them out of it. Weasels have a tendency to do that in any situation, which makes them natural lawyers.

But Ziggy and Rocco were also clever. They never got

into fights where they didn't have some advantage over their opponents, whether it was knowing the layout of a rumble, having the right tools for the job, or whatever. It's almost funny how they got offed by a bunch of students in a random brawl. I allow myself a little, rueful smile. I'd always hoped I'd be the one to put them in the Pound once and for all, but I guess I'll never have that opportunity, now that they're being fitted for wooden overcoats.

"What about Ayani?" I would have asked, but the question doesn't even pass my throat. I notice that the music's stopped, and a quiet tension seeps into my stomach. I hastily stuff the notepad into my pocket and sit on my hands again. The badger outside the room pushes the curtain aside with a thick, meaty paw, barely even registering that Ramona is still dressed and sitting next to me.

"Time's up, sir," he says, almost robotically with the number of times he's probably said it tonight. "Thank you for visiting."

"He's paid for another dance, Tristram," says Ramona. The badger looks a bit annoyed by this but sighs knowingly.

"Okay, Mona," he says. "But remember, Jock don't pay extra for you to shake your ass twice in a row. And we need you back on bar when you're done."

Tristram disappears through the bead curtain. Once he's safely out of sight, Ramona looks at me and winks, the tiny bead of light that is her eye flickering in the gloom, a single dainty finger on her lips.

"Enjoy it," she whispers coquettishly. "This one's on me."

She gets up and starts dancing again. I sit, I watch, I enjoy the show, and I think I may be in way over my head with what I know now. I'm halfway home before I realize that I hadn't paid for a single thing at the club all night, and it's a pleasant surprise, but it does nothing to ease my troubled thoughts.

Having not had a drink since concluding my business at the Watering Hole only a couple of hours ago, I sit at my desk and pour myself some whiskey into the little glass that probably hasn't been washed in ages, noting how far down the bottle I've gone. It's been a long day, and I need some liquid refreshment, and, in my opinion, I've more than earned it. It's also been a day of many surprises and revelations, so much so that I ruffle the fur between my pointed ears in frustration. My client is going to lose some sort of standing if I screw up. I've made a promise to an ox who's as sharp as a bowling ball to do right by his fallen brother. I know the names of the dead from the fight, and a raccoon stripper who's smarter than she looks seems to have taken a shine to my spur-of-the-moment false identity, or maybe just to me in general. On top of all that, my target, Ayani Onyelé, is still as elusive as ever, and that's the point that irritates me the most.

I sip at the glass, the fire-water burning away the mental fatigue I'm feeling, and I ponder, as I always do when too much has taken place in one day, scribbling a few notes while they're still fresh in my head and undiluted by booze. Ayani is still elusive, true, but I'm getting more background about her family, and the position they might be in. Influential, wealthy, probably ruled by protocol and etiquette. If Ayani's place of employment says anything about her, she must have been choking under the yoke of formality, dying to get out. Must be the wild-child of the family.

Speaking of dying, it still irks me that Ziggy and Rocco are dead, especially at the hands of a bunch of drunken frat-boys. I never liked those dogs, but it had been a goal in my life to ship them off to the Pound for good. Bill said to me that his brother had noticed their interest in Ayani. Something sinister hangs around that piece of information, so I note it down. Jock could be right, that they were just there to put pressure on him for more protection money, but something still raises my dander about it. That's just too damn simple. I reach into a box on my desk and stuff a dog biscuit into my mouth, crunching it hurriedly so as not to lose my train of thought.

I remember the names of those cats, too. I open a desk drawer and pull out a phone book, the Oldsburg Telephone Directory, and flick through to the business pages. Just as I thought, they were from pretty rich families. The Arden kid was probably from the family behind Arden Shipping. Lynns Steel Mills is in the book, too, as well as Sullivan Plaza Hotels. Rich kids all, with not a lick of sense between them when they decided to take on known packsters. I sigh at the waste of life, even the lives of cats. I put the book back in its drawer, somberly, and shake my head slowly. It's not relevant as far as I know, but it's still tragic.

I swallow what remains of the biscuit and pull the driver's license that I swiped from the diner out of my pocket. Benjamin Orcowitz. This ass must have seen something that night, maybe where Ayani escaped to. I need to find this guy and get him to spill what he knows. As stubborn as donkeys and their ilk are, it could be important. I stare at the plastic card in my hand, and the tiny photo of Orcowitz stares back, sullen and quiet. I should probably hit the Easttown docks tomorrow. There's likely to be more than a dozen shipping companies there, but it narrows the search by a big margin. The card still smells faintly of the sea, despite having been carried around by yours truly for several hours.

I yawn widely, the tiredness setting in, my tongue curling like most dogs. How long has it been since I slept in my own bed? I know I can just fold it out of the wall, but that requires clearing some space on the floor, something I really don't have the energy for right now. I slouch my hat over my eyes, put my feet on my desk, and quietly drift to sleep.

I know this place. I'm at Sam's Bar & Grill, with its green neon lights over the bar, the false Shamrock, liquor bottles lining the shelves, and the constant haze of smoke. I know these people, too: Tilton's here, and Jen, and Bose, and Tony Henderson, but there are many others I don't know. Why's Tony wearing his dress uniform? Oh, wait, now I know. It's like that time... Tilton's wearing a black armband on that horrible suit of his. Jen is wearing a long, black dress and has her face covered by a black veil to hide the tears she's shedding. The crowd of animals forms around the bar, and I'm among them, dragged along for the ride.

Commissioner Talbot is here too, his owl head turning majestically as he gives a eulogy that's being drowned out by the thudding bass of dance music. This isn't how things are supposed to be at all. I know. I was there. Why am I here? In a panic, I look around me to see if I can recognize anyone else. There's a zebra here, wearing one of the grotesque, wooden ceremony masks of their homeland. Tilton never wore a suit back then, either, because he wasn't a detective. Beside him, Vincent Bose, that damned hyena, is cackling like a madman, even though I know he held his tongue on that day. I spot Amber in the crowd, one of her eyes black and swollen, thick make-up barely concealing the bruises and scars all over her face, like somebody had taken a golf club to her. The scent of rotting fruit is everywhere, sickly and cloying. This doesn't make any sense!

Then it hits me. Behind Talbot, laid across the bar, stark as a monolith, is a coffin. Black pine, with silver fittings, just like the one *he* was buried in. A black and white framed picture of *him* is resting atop the lid, along with *his* cap and badge. Ursine Officer 5981. My old partner. The lid creaks open, deafening against the surreal, energetic stillness of everything around me. Then, a voice pierces my mind, hollow and echoing like obsidian bells dropped into a cave.

"Why wasn't it you?" it says. I try to scream, desperately wanting to get away from the madness, when I realize my mouth has been sewn shut.

I wake with a start, my thrashing feet scattering bottle caps and biscuit crumbs into the piles of trash all around me, my hat flopping pathetically onto the floor beside my desk. Another damn nightmare about him. I know I should let it go, but it's always there, hanging over my shoulder like a phantom. I look up to check the filthy clock on the opposite wall from my desk. It's thirteen minutes past seven and still surprisingly dark outside. I assure myself it was just a nightmare, nothing to worry about. Today is Friday, after all. Do I go, or do I not? I still don't know. He was my partner, after all. It's at that point I look, half-asleep, at my desk. I see the plastic license there in front of me, almost like it's staring at me. Shit. Got to see to that later. That'll be my first call today, but I need to clean myself up.

I get up from the chair, my knees creaking as I stand. I really need to lose weight. I shake my head a bit to lose the grogginess, and haul myself to the bathroom. A shower would do me a world of good, especially with the weird, itchy feeling I can still feel around my lips. Nightmare or not, that's pretty damn traumatic. Why do I have those dreams? Guilt, maybe? The thoughts exit my mind as I turn on the faucet, the water flowing out icy cold, followed by boiling hot, then a nice equilibrium. At least the damn thing isn't spewing out brown water this time. Thank St Roch for small mercies.

I throw off the clothes I hadn't realized I'd been wearing for three days, giving them a cursory sniff. Ugh... Looks like I'll need to hit the laundromat at some point soon. It's then that I look at myself — really look at myself — in the bathroom mirror, leaning on the sink, the flickering bulb above my head casting long shadows over my face. When did I get so old and fat? Yeah, it's still me in the frame, but where did that youthful cadet with his tin badge go? No use wondering about it now, after everything. The youthful pup is an old boy these days, and the badge is safely locked away in a drawer. I sigh quietly to myself before stepping gingerly into the shower, the hot water washing over me like a rainstorm. Something deep down tells me that this is what I really needed. The warmth of the water soaks through my fur to the skin. I brush myself all over with my hands, and an assortment of biscuit crumbs and loose hairs come toppling down into the drain. Wonder how many of those hairs used to belong to that raccoon girl? Eduardo is gonna kill me for that if it clogs up, but I don't care. I feel clean, for the first time in ages, without the sleaze and the smog and the grime of this city on my body. Clean, like I'm a good animal again. It's a strange and unfamiliar feeling, but not unwelcome.

Once I finish showering and shake myself dry, I find

myself a clean shirt and suit, a tasteful grey combo. That ought to help too, I think; be professional and clean about everything, and you'll get further than you expected. I pick up my hat, the old fedora I've had since I started this little agency, and dust it off, too. As I rise, I pause at my desk drawer. I unlock it, the key stiff in my fingers, and look inside, the tin badge looking back up at me. Canine Officer 7832, Oldsburg City Police Department, it proudly proclaims on the shield.

To Serve and Protect.

I smile grimly at my old companion that I'd worn so many times on the beat, and at the .38 service revolver beside it, unused for years. I pull the weapon from the drawer carefully, cradling it in my hands like something precious, the oiled metal of the barrel cold in my grip. Maybe I'm going to need this from here on out, especially if the packs are involved. I'll need more protection than my stunner if they catch on to my investigation, if they're involved at all. I swing the chambers out, checking to see that they're loaded. Still full, just as I'd left it. I also dig out my old shoulder-holster and slip into it, a tight fit given my waistline these days. It's uncomfortable but necessary. It wouldn't do for me to be flashing a gat around openly. What would Mr. Pettibone say to that, I wonder? I chuckle at the thought, knowing that tight-ass would probably flip his lid. Guess it's only natural to think ill of someone who rubs you the wrong way.

It's just after eight a.m., and the sunlight is starting to filter in through the blinds. Feeling much more comfortable and well-armed, I put on my suit jacket and trench coat before exiting my apartment, heading for the docks. I secretly hope today goes smoother than yesterday, but I'm not holding my breath.

* * *

The sun is shining weakly through the oily, grey clouds covering the city by the time I reach my destination. It's been years since I was in Easttown, but not much has changed in all that time. The district is heavily industrialized, as ever it was, refineries and factories belching out smoke from their chimneys, with ships bringing in the raw materials that fuel the fires of big business. It's just as grimy and dull as you'd imagine, and everywhere there's always somebody that needs to be doing something or going someplace, the working stiffs with calloused hands that punch in before the rest of Oldsburg is awake and punch out long after everyone is asleep. If the Law is an animal, then Industry has to be a universal constant, like death or taxes. Without it, modern society grinds to a halt, and then we're no better than the savage beasts our ancestors were thousands of years ago.

But it's not the factories and workshops that interest me; it's the docks. I scrunch my hands into my coat pockets to keep out the still present chill of the morning air, and stride purposefully in that direction. My best bet would be to talk to the harbormaster. He's likely to know most of the folk that work here, and I still have Orcowitz's license in my pocket. I can present it to him as a 'concerned citizen', say that I found it and wanted to get it back to its rightful owner in person, which is at least partially true. It'd probably save me some time over asking around, and it'd keep my motives secret.

The offices of the Port Authority aren't difficult to find, situated right in the center of the harbor district, nestled among the huge warehouses and stacks of shipping containers that are omnipresent here. It's a large, unassuming, two-story building, with whitewashed concrete walls gradually staining yellow from the sea breezes and the pall of pollution from the surrounding area. There's an intercom next to the heavy-duty steel door. I push the button, and a faint buzz sounds from the little box. I wait a few seconds before somebody answers.

"Port Authority, how can I help you?" comes a thoroughly bored female voice over the scratchy sound system. I turn on the innocence.

"Uh, hi," I say. "I'd like to talk to the harbormaster? If that's okay?"

"What business, sir?" The voice responds, primly.

"I need to ask him about someone who works here," I reply. "I think I have something that belongs to them."

There's a pause for a moment. I wait with bated breath.

"All right, sir. The door's unlocked," says the female voice. "You can come in."

I breathe a sigh of relief that I hadn't realized I'd been holding, and turn the handle, stepping into the cool murkiness of the hallway before me. This was easier than I could have imagined. I'm greeted by a flight of metal steps right in front of me, and to my right I see a gaggle of lackeys running too-and-fro arranging the paperwork on this level, a rusty old fan creaking half-heartedly as it spins slowly overhead. The harbormaster isn't here, I figure, so I climb the steel steps to the upper floor. He wouldn't get his feathers dirty with the menial tasks that can so easily be shoved onto the lower ranks.

My steps echo quietly as I ascend the stairs. I find the harbormaster's office at the top, an ostentatious hardwood door with gaudy gilt lettering, surrounded by wall-to-wall carpeting in a garish paisley design, and kitschy ornaments, much at odds with the hustle and dilapidation that I'd seen downstairs. Squalor obviously can't climb, but bad taste goes where it pleases. The door proudly states itself to be the office of Francis Eames, Harbormaster, and to the left of that is his secretary's desk, the intercom button lying close to her typewriter. She's a duck, wearing horn-rimmed glasses and a polka-dot polyester dress. I wouldn't have guessed from our earlier conversation that she was a duck, as she's lost that characteristic, slurping lisp that her species tends to have. I tip my hat to her, and she acknowledges my presence, wearing a sour expression as she types, the ink-ribbon jamming occasionally, followed by a quiet curse or possibly a quack. There are a couple seats nearby, so I lay myself heavily into one of them. Let me tell you, the padding on those chairs is purely for show. I've never sat down on anything so uncomfortable in my life, and that's saying something.

Soon enough, the hardwood door opens, and I'm met by harbormaster Eames, a gull with a few too many meals behind him, if his gut tells me anything, barely contained within a poorly tailored suit. He ushers me into his office, also decked out in tacky ornamentation, and I present the card to him. I play up the concerned citizen act for all its worth, with him sat at his desk, sucking his teeth and scratching his chin, until he finally remembers where I need to go, giving me a location. It's kind of approximate, as he knows as much about the goings-on around here as I do, but the face of a donkey isn't forgotten quickly. He points me towards Pier 12. To his knowledge, he'd seen a lot of donkeys around that area of the docks, longshoremen and stevedores going about the business of loading and unloading cargo. I thank him and show myself out.

Pier 12, even at this point in the day, is a riot of activity. Despite the cool breezes coming in from off-shore and the chilly spring air, it's almost oppressively hot and smoky in this part of the docklands, with all the heavy machinery rumbling around, belching clouds of exhaust fumes and heat into the atmosphere. The unmistakable scents of diesel oil, rust, and sea salt hang heavily in the air, intermingled with the brackish undercurrent of the sludge that collects at the bottom of boats. The creaking and groaning of machinery long past any kind of maintenance date forms a symphony with the roar of engines and the shouts of the dockworkers, the slapping of the waves on the pier all but drowned out. It's a dirty place, full of dirty jobs, but somebody has to do them, and I really don't envy the dirty animals who do. Everywhere I look, another anonymous, oil-smudged face looks back, briefly and gloomily, before their eyes turn downward and they get back to whatever they were doing. If this is an honest day's work, it's no wonder so many, turn to crime.

Rising above the morass of industry all around stands a huge warehouse, painted a deep red, with a familiar name: Arden Shipping Ltd. *Funny*, I think to myself. It's either got some connection to what I already know, which I dismiss with healthy skepticism, or it's just a bizarre coincidence. I pull a cigarette from my pocket and am just in the process of lighting it when I'm stopped by someone shouting at me from across the dock. My ears prick up, and I see a rhino stomping towards me, disgruntled, a hard hat on his head, his employee I.D. tag flapping heavily against his visibility vest. Wouldn't like to be on the end of that horn, let me tell you.

"Put that cigarette out!" He bellows at me. "D'you know

how much gasoline is around here? You wanna blow us all to hell?"

I quickly pocket my lighter, snuffing out the flame, the unlit cigarette dangling from my lips. I glance at his tag. He's the foreman.

"Sorry, buddy," I start, "I didn't realize…"

"No, you didn't realize," he says to me, sarcastic and furious. "What are you doing here anyway, wise guy?"

"Looking for one of your crew," I say curtly, getting to the point as quickly as I can. "Benjamin Orcowitz. Know where I can find him?"

"He's on a smoke break," says the rhino, his horned face swinging back to the activity on the docks. "Shelter's on the other side of the warehouse. And tell that bum to get back to work when you see 'im!"

He stops paying attention to me and goes back to bellowing orders at his subordinates. I quietly take my leave and head in the direction of the Arden Shipping warehouse, the hubbub gradually receding behind me. It's still a mess of rusted containers and old smells around me, but I follow the trail of tobacco smoke, picking it out of the insane mess of scents behind me. Not long into my search, I spot the Perspex and steel shelter ahead of me, at the extreme side of the Arden warehouse. I figure I'm far enough away from anything flammable that I light up and keep an eye on the occupants of the shelter. Many of the windows have seen the pen of some graffiti artist over the years, but I can still see who's in there. A bulldog, a warthog, and a donkey.

Benjamin Orcowitz. He's smoking his cigarette and twitching like he knows someone's coming for him, furtively glancing around. It can't be me he's on the lookout for, surely?

Then he lifts his heavy eyes in my direction, and they widen for just a second, the cigarette dangling in his fingers, halfway to his lips. There's a timeless moment where we see each other as we are, the world around us seeming to slow to a crawl. Time suddenly catches up, though, and he bolts for the exit to the shelter, knocking his smoking companions aside, the cigarette flying from his hand. Dammit. I throw my own smoke away and give chase.

My cop instincts immediately kick in, and my legs start pumping faster than they have in years, but I'm on his home turf. He's got me at a disadvantage. He hops a bundle of pipes, and I keep right on his tail, catching my toe on the obstacle, but steadying myself with practiced ease. A right turn sees him nimbly dodging pallets of oil drums, and I follow as fast as I can, but not before thudding into one particularly heavy barrel. Though this winds me for a second, I keep on his tail. He's still in my sight until he takes a left turn. Blindly, I follow him, between the echoing canyons of storage containers, only to see he's gone. There aren't many exits for him. He'll either have to double back somehow, or come into my crosshairs to make a break for it. Fortunately for me, he stupidly chooses the latter. As I'm stood wondering where he might be, catching my breath, he springs out into my field of view, and I pick up the chase, my stubby legs working like pistons behind him. A crack of daylight shows, and he breaks for the wide-open space. My lungs are burning by the time I reach that gap, but I really need to catch this guy.

Once I get out of the claustrophobic atmosphere of the containers, I look around, panting. He's racing down the waterfront, pretty fast for one of his species. He's shoving dockworkers aside like ragdolls in his panic, many able to catch themselves, others sent sprawling on the concrete, and at least one splashing down into the indescribable muck of the bay below. I pull my piece, just in case, thundering towards him. I'm more than prepared to fire a couple of warning shots if I have to, but I don't want to injure the guy or risk injuring anybody else in the crossfire.

The security gates to Pier 12 are right in front of us, and he puts on one last burst of speed. I swear quietly under my heaving breath and double my efforts, my finger still on the trigger. I hear a few startled gasps and cries as I shove my way past, but I pay no heed, concentrating solely on Orcowitz. Then I notice he's limping, his pace slowing. He must have twisted his ankle or something when I lost track of him. He's tiring, and I'm within reaching distance. Touching distance. I can smell the fear radiating from him, like feeling heat from a fire. I throw my entire weight onto him, tackling him to the ground. I guess playing little-league football as a pup was good for something. We crash into a tangle of limbs before I reinforce my control on the situation. I pin his hands at his back with my free hand and snarl as best I can, my teeth flashing white.

"Why…" I pant heavily between breaths, "… did you… run?"

"You're here to kill me, aren't you?" Orcowitz replies, gasping for breath himself, his voice muffled against the floor. This takes me aback for a moment, but I compose myself, and I definitely don't let go of his wrists.

"I'm not out to kill you, buddy," I say to him, my breath still sharp and painful in my lungs, like a cheese grater over slate. "If I really wanted to kill you, I would've offed you in the shelter, and your buddies, too. Remote location, no witnesses, industrial mishap on the certificates of death. Made it look like an accident."

"You can't do that!" He cries out in protest, still struggling against my grip. "What about the cops? You'd never get away with it!"

Stubborn as always. Typical of his species. He's avoiding everything but me. The fact that I just told him how he could die — even though I was bluffing — is insignificant compared to the lumpen Corgi ass on top of him. I sheathe the revolver and slowly extricate myself from him, taking care that he doesn't try to run again. It's a trust thing. He flips over quickly, his nostrils flaring wide from lack of breath, but soon we've got eye contact, and he softens up a touch. It's then he drops the bomb.

"Wait a minute," he says. "You're not with the packs, are you?"

I'm dragging Benjamin back to somewhere we can talk privately. He says he prefers to be called Benny, but I'm still going to call him Benjamin for the shit he just put me through. He's still limping, worse than before. Probably didn't help any when I clobbered him. We decide against the smoking shelter. His little scene has made people jumpy, and it's far too public a place. There's a greasy, beat-up old burger van by the docks, someplace that private business can be carried out, especially if you stay out of sight and hand the staff a few bills.

We approach, ordering separately. I keep my eye on him, ready to pounce if he even thinks of running. Not that he really can, given his ankle. Not entirely sure how I can justify that to the gathering of hungry dockers, either, but I'm pretty sure he can't find a reasonable excuse for bolting unexplained from a crowd in the first place. The horse in the van, his face pale and drawn from too many nights sleeping in that rusty box, hands me my change, and I nod to Orcowitz. He acknowledges the nod, and we slip inconspicuously behind the burger van, just out of sight, but not out of hearing range, just in case anyone gets suspicious. He's got his handful of fries and I my burger. I've no intention of eating the thing, just from the way it smells: dehydrated onions, stale bread, and highly questionable meat, probably processed somewhere with worse hygiene standards than a truck-stop bathroom. Still, it's best to keep up appearances so nobody gets too curious.

"Okay, Benjamin," I begin. "Why are the packs after you?"

"First things first, pal," he snorts back. "Mind telling me who you are and why you were chasing me?"

I sigh, frustrated. It's probably best to be upfront with the guy.

"I'm a private investigator," I say. "That's all you need to know about me. As for why I was chasing you, I'm working a case, and your name kept coming up, so to speak. I've got a few questions to ask you, is all. You answer them well, you'll never see me again."

I notice the slight nervous twitch of his ears, and he starts chewing idly on the fries. If he knew how old and dirty the grease was on those things, he'd probably think twice about it, but I keep that bit of information to myself.

"How do I know I can trust you?" Benjamin asks, tiny crumbs of potato falling from between his teeth to roll down his grubby shirt. I flash the shoulder-holster, and he pauses, stunned, before I quickly close my jacket again.

"The fact that I haven't plugged you yet should be a good

indicator, jackass. And it's bad manners to talk with your mouth full," I snarl. I don't usually go in for speciesist slurs, but it seems to get the point across. He gulps heavily, partly to swallow the foul fries he's been snacking on and partly from the intimidation.

"So... uh..." he begins nervously. "... the packs, right?"

"Yes, Benjamin, the packs," I repeat patiently. "Why do you think they're after you?"

"Well, uh... It all started when the boss called me into his office..." he says.

"The boss?" I ask. "As in your foreman? Or the harbormaster?"

"No, man," he says, shaking his bristly mane excitedly, "I mean the *boss*, as in Mr. Arden! He wanted to talk to me!"

This statement strikes me as odd. Conroy Arden is infamously reclusive, content to run his shipping empire in solitude from his office building in the Financial District. Nobody ever sees him coming or going from that building, only the pristine black sedan with dark-tinted windows that he's always chauffeured around in. The tabloids and gossip pages always have a field day speculating what it is he gets up to in private, everything from writing his memoirs and fruitlessly practicing his golf swing to pissing in old coffee cans while wearing a tinfoil hat, but nobody could ever tell for sure. He also hasn't been photographed in years, ever since his wife died in that boating accident, which was when his period of isolation began. Does he even know one of his sons is dead? What would that even do to the guy? Whatever the case may be, him wanting to speak to a complete nobody like Benjamin sounds fishy. I think I should press the issue, just to make sure he isn't yanking my chain. Needless to say, I don't hold my breath.

"You mean Conroy Arden," I say incredulously. "*The* Conroy Arden summoned you up to talk with him?"

"Yeah, man!" the donkey says, the unusual light of self-assurance glowing in his eyes. "He talked to me!"

"Okay, okay," I say to him, his enthusiasm not rubbing off on me. "What did he want to talk to you about?"

At this, he goes strangely quiet, thinking, still munching the fries and leaning against the van to give his bad ankle a rest.

"He... he wanted me to do something for him... quiet-like... something he couldn't trust his security guys with," he says, a twinge of guilt edging his words. A crisis of conscience, maybe?

"What did he want you to do?" I ask.

"Mr. Arden wanted me to look after Danny," Orcowitz says. "He said he was worried about him but that his guards would look too suspicious. Said he needed some unknown to do it. Said he'd been getting threats from someone about the kid, I dunno. He was kinda vague on the details, just said he'd pay me big to keep an eye on the boy."

At this point, Benjamin resignedly dunks his fries into a trash bin beside him, probably thinking better of continuing his impromptu meal. Maybe the grease has gotten to him. Or could it be something else? I've got to know more.

"What else did he tell you?" I ask, putting my hand in my pocket for my cigarettes. I rattle the box. Sounds like only a couple are left. I'll need to get some more on the way back to the apartment.

"I don't remember too well, man," he says. "I was almost shitting bricks; I was that frightened!"

"Try," I say firmly. "Anything you can remember could help me to help you." I pluck one of the two cigarettes left in the pack and stick it in my mouth, since I had to throw the previous one away to chase this ass. I guess there's no harm lighting up here. We're far enough away from any machinery to be safe, though there might be the remote risk of a grease fire. Orcowitz's brow knits in thought, his eyes screwed up tight like he's thinking real hard about his meeting with Arden.

"Something about if I didn't, then being fired would be the least of my worries? I think that's what scared me, man," he says, finally. "I thought he was just being crazy, like the papers say he is, but there was something in his voice that really frightened me… like I was going to die if I failed…"

I notice his hands trembling. I also notice I'm barely into my smoke, and, annoyingly, my better instincts kick in. I take the cigarette from my mouth and offer him the rest of it.

"I think you need this more than I do," I say to him, not unkindly. Orcowitz takes the smoldering cigarette without question, his stubby fingers still shuddering, and takes a long drag. He's still tense, but the nicotine hit seems to have helped. *I've really got to stop giving these things out*, I think to myself. *The expense is killing me!* After a couple of minutes, once he's finished the last few scraps of tobacco, he stamps the butt out on the floor gingerly with his gimpy leg.

"I saw Danny die…" he says. "In the fight at that club in Coldwater. Those Dobermans killed him. Danny stabbed one of them in the eye… with a comb! A *fucking comb*, man!"

"Calm down," I say softly, trying to keep him from drawing attention. "Tell me what you saw that night. Why were you there? Looking after Danny?"

He breathes in heavily, composing himself. This is what I

need to know, and I can't risk this donkey losing his cool or causing a commotion.

"Yeah, I was there keeping an eye on Danny," Benjamin finally says, his composure returned. "Mr. Arden's people got in contact with me saying his son and a few other boys were hitting up the Watering Hole that evening. I live near there, anyway, in Coldwater, so I said I'd drop in and quietly keep an eye out. I ain't one to turn down a beer, especially if the head honcho's paying for it.

"Anyway, I saw them come in. They sat at a table near the main stage. There were these three dogs in suits at a table nearby, and they just started staring at each other. Like really glaring, man. Then Danny and his buddies started ordering shots, about two dozen between them. They got pretty hammered. Then one of the Dobermans stuck his foot out when the zebra waitress was walking past. She fell flat on her face, spilled the next round of drinks all over Danny and his buddies. That must have pissed them off because one of the other boys flipped the table over. They squared off with those dogs, like those prize-fighters you see in boxing? I thought it was just going to be some pushing and shoving... then the claws came out, and... well... they started clawing and biting... killing each other... then I ran..."

That set the scene for me more clearly. Ayani had been in the middle of the floor when the fight broke out. She could have easily been killed there and then, but Amber's story had disabused me of that notion as she hadn't seen Ayani anywhere among the dead, and I knew there hadn't been any zebra blood spilled at the scene, or I'd have smelled it. I feel like I'm getting closer to finding out what happened, but I need something more solid to work from.

"What happened to the waitress? The zebra serving Danny and his buddies," I ask. "Did you notice what happened to her?"

Benjamin thinks for a few seconds. I wait, tucking my hands into my coat pockets for warmth. In this line of work, you learn to be patient with certain animals. He finally answers.

"I remember… this cobra started hissing in her face, man. Guess he musta been pretty drunk too. Then the bouncer came and started dragging him off the dancefloor. There were two others with him. Cobras, I mean. When the fight started, they all got involved. I think I saw that zebra run for it, into the back somewhere. I wasn't really paying much attention, just trying to save my own skin, man."

Finally! A breakthrough! I'd been looking in the wrong place the whole time. Ayani hadn't headed for the front doors like everyone else; she'd headed for the back. She probably didn't want to get caught by anyone, especially the police, given her circumstances. I secretly smile to myself, but one final detail needs to be addressed.

"One last thing… what made you think I was with the packs?" I ask, genuinely curious as to what the answer would be.

"You've read the papers, man," says Benjamin. "Mr. Arden is in bed with those animals. He'd have me whacked by them for sure. A dog in a suit shows up at my workplace? What else was I supposed to think?"

"I'm not even sure Mr. Arden knows his son is dead," I retort. "Besides, you ought to know better than to trust the newspapers in this city. Anyway, take care of yourself, Benny."

I shake the donkey's hand and turn away, heading for the

gates of Pier 12. In Benny's hand, I've left my last cigarette, and his vehicle license wrapped up in a $20 bill. The expense is really killing me.

I've picked up another pack of smokes by the time I get back to my apartment, along with today's paper. There are a few things I need to check, even if the information is barely reliable. Today, I'm not jumping straight to the sports pages like I always do (the Bluesocks are having a terrible season, anyway), but rather looking for the obituaries and funeral announcements. Barely glancing up from my study of the pages, I reach for the bottle of bourbon on my desk and pour myself a glass, the motions as fluid, absent, and seamless as a reflex action, while my eyes keep scanning. A lot of cases of truly aged animals shuffling off the mortal coil in this edition, but a few younger types, too. It especially breaks my heart to see puppies in these columns, but there are a couple to see. Cycle of life, right? I pick up the tumbler and idly sip at the liquor, the familiar hit washing through me.

Sure enough, Daniel Arden's name is in the paper. The announcement takes up a good portion of the text. The funeral is scheduled for Monday morning at Shady Oaks cemetery. That place is some high-class real-estate just outside of town, and I'd expect nothing less from a business empire like Arden Shipping. Rodney Lynns and Toby Sullivan are also mentioned in their own entries, and scheduled for the two days following, but it'll be Daniel's funeral that I think the media circus is going to swarm around, given his father's eccentricities. I keep reading, not expecting to see much else, before putting the paper aside on my cluttered desk and lighting up a smoke from the new pack. For some reason, I find myself staring at that old wall clock, the hands ticking away slowly, oblivious to the comings and goings of the world around it. It's coming up to the early afternoon. I sit, and I smoke, and I drink some more, and I ponder.

From what Benny told me, Ayani had probably slipped out of a rear exit on the night of the brawl. That gives me somewhere to start, and I note it down in my book. The club won't be open for hours, and that gives me plenty of time to sniff around back. It's possible she could have dropped something or damaged something, or left some other kind of trail for me to follow, something the CSI boys had missed, especially since they'd been preoccupied with the main room. The only snag in that plan is that it's rained recently, so it'll be difficult to track by scent, but if I can find any kind of physical evidence, that'd be enough to start with.

I shuffle in my chair, trying to get comfortable, and take another sip of whiskey. I notice that the cigarette is burning low in my fingers, so I reach across my desk for the ashtray and stub it out. I briefly glance down at the folded newspaper. The headline is something about an ambassador's reception last night. Maybe that's the 'function' Ziva had attended. It certainly seems like her kind of thing. I make a mental note to give her a call at some point to tell her about my progress with the case and request more funds; I'd rather she didn't send her little raccoon-servant to grill me again. Not too soon, though. I'm still running on speculation and witness statements so far, and I need something solid to show for my efforts.

Then, of course, there are the threats that were made to Conroy Arden about his son. Benny was vague about it, but there might be some connection, even if it is a tenuous one. I'll need to see if I can get any more reliable information about it from the people at Arden Shipping, but I'm not holding out much hope. Information that sensitive would probably be unobtainable, or even make me some serious enemies if I conduct myself poorly, though I don't think Arden is in with the packs, as Benny posited. I chuckle at the thought, mainly because I'm starting to sound like that know-it-all Pettibone. Still, it's something I need to handle carefully.

As a last resort, I could make some quiet inquiries at the University. Daniel and his friends were students there, and they probably talked about their problems to their classmates or the other players on the basketball team. It's not even beyond the bounds of possibility that somebody might have seen a few shady characters on campus. Ziggy and Rocco always had a habit of making an impact wherever they went, whether it was a wise decision or not. I note down that plan on my notepad.

As I'm writing, I suddenly start hearing thumping from upstairs, alongside orgasmic moaning and a mule braying. Oh no. Eduardo got himself a date for the day. I'd better leave while the getting's good. I finish the last drop of bourbon in the glass, get up from my chair, put on my coat and hat, stuff my notepad in my pocket, and get out of my apartment as quickly and quietly as I can manage. I've got places to be other than here, anyway.

Coldwater during the day is definitely a lot less threatening than at night. Though I'm still expecting to be harangued by a passing drunk or junkie or vagrant, the area's overall seediness has dropped by a huge margin, but that really isn't saying a lot. A sewer pipe could burst into the street, or a house fire could start spontaneously, and it'd probably be an improvement to the neighborhood.

I avoid eye contact with anyone on the streets until I'm finally at the back alley behind the Watering Hole. It's pretty much your run-down alley; you've seen one, you've seen them all. Thick, grey steam spews from vents in the neighboring buildings. Newspaper sheets scud across the concrete, their headlines bleached and long-forgotten, whatever front-page political figure having long passed into obscurity. The smell of trash is terrible, a mixture of booze and disinfectant almost masking everything else. It's definitely not going to be easy finding a scent against the background odor and the recent weather, but I might strike it lucky. Something also tells me that the garbage-men don't come around too often, maybe once a week or less, so the two dumpsters lining the walls might also be helpful.

I start at the back door, a sickly odor flooding my nose, a mixture of chemicals, body oil, and assorted sweat permeating beyond the exit. There are so many different species mixed together. Jock must hire a lot of talent to appeal to as wide an audience as he can muster. As much as I sniff around, it's difficult drawing a bead on one specific scent. I try to focus and weed out anything that isn't relevant. There are several smells that I can instantly rule out: badger, deer, rabbit, raccoon. For some reason, my mind wanders back to that Ramona girl, but I squash the memory back into my subconscious. I home in on the equine scents, and I smell zebra. It's faint, but it's there, definitely a few days old and tinged with the unmistakable musk of fear. Not too far away, and following the trail, I find a partial bloody handprint on one of the dumpsters, though it's not her blood. From how bitter and familiar it smells, I'd guess the blood once belonged to Hank, at least after he had been bitten.

I check over the dumpster for anything else that could easily be missed. The partial print is under the rim, so it mostly avoided being washed away by the rain. My brow furrows. There's something that I'm overlooking, I'm sure of it. I stand dumbfounded for a second or two, idly reaching for my smokes until I realize I'd left them on my desk at home. Dammit, Eduardo. I know he's not going to smoke them, because he doesn't bother the tenants of his building unless he's got some sort of beef with them (which, to be fair, is a lot of the time), but he never enters someone's apartment unannounced, or if they're not home. The ass has a few redeeming qualities, discretion being one of them, but that still doesn't amount to a hill of beans. This is an inconvenience I could have done without. Maybe there are a few half-smoked ends in the trash I could…

Then, like a bolt from the blue, I think to look *inside* the dumpster, and can't believe it took me this long to think to do that. As I heft the sun-bleached plastic lid upwards, at about my eye level, the smell of old, stale booze amplifies a hundred-fold, but so do two other scents; blood and a memorable, oddly pleasant sensation. Pheromones. There's something in there, I know it! Checking to make sure I'm not being watched, I flip the lid of the dumpster back until it touches the wall with no danger of it closing on me, and I clumsily climb up the side, the soles of my shoes skidding on the slick surface as I do. I make a cursory scan of the inside to see a mess of lumpy trash bags. There are probably a lot of bottles in there, so it'd be a dumb decision to climb in and root around, but I really don't have a choice. I can't let whatever is in there be collected on trash day. I pull myself up and vault in, being careful to land on my feet as I do, some of the bags closing around my ankles.

I hear a lot of crunching and cracking, and confirm to myself that, yes, a dumpster behind a bar would definitely be full of broken glass. This one has something inside it that could prove useful to me, though, so I squat down among the bags, sniffing here and there, trying to pick up on the pheromone scent that I know so well, delicately shuffling any sacks aside that I feel I can safely handle. As I do, the smell of blood and cobra venom gets stronger until I find the source. Half-buried among the stacks of old bottles lies a crumpled, brown paper bag with rusty stains on it that I know only too well from experience. Dried blood. There's something covered in blood in there.

I carefully move aside a trash bag full of glass that's pinning the package down and slowly begin to pick it up, cautious about how I shift my ungainly weight. Every fiber of my being tenses like a spring as I curl my fingers further into the tan-colored paper. Suddenly, something gives way under my left foot, and I stumble, surprised, still gripping the bag. To my horror, the trash bag I'd moved aside only recently topples onto my right arm with a crunch, and I feel a dozen or more shards of glass dig into the back of my hand through the plastic, though my coat manages to save the rest of my arm. I panic and yelp in pain, yanking my hand out, causing more of a gash as the glass tears at my skin. My prize is still clutched in my hand, and I notice I'm bleeding from several shallow cuts, alongside a couple of deeper ones. I quickly pass the paper bag into my undamaged hand, so as not to contaminate whatever is inside and instinctively go to lick my lacerated paw. I'm dissuaded from this notion as I notice the fragments of glass that are stuck there, stinging like a swarm of wasps. I sniff, and my heart freezes in terror as I realize there are traces of leftover venom on my hand. This place is frequented by snakes... Oh, St Roch, *no*!

I hurriedly and painfully drag myself out of the dumpster, landing hard on the ground in my haste, knees cracking and buckling. I grit my teeth and grunt in pain, both from the glass in my hand and the grating of my knees from the crash landing, but I've got to get this seen to immediately. I quickly flip the lid closed on the dumpster with a loud thud and set to hurry off before anyone notices me, wrapping my paw in a sheet of clean-looking newspaper from the floor. The smell of my own blood starts mingling with the putrid stink of the alley and the poisonous elements in my hand, and my mind starts racing in a cold panic.

Wait... Jerome. Yes! His place is in Coldwater, and it's not too far away. He can fix this. He has to!

My eyes are blurry by the time I reach the clinic, though I don't know if that's from the venom or from the pain of my aching knees. It's a brick building, well-kept, unlike most of the others in Coldwater. A huge marquee above the door announces it as the Coldwater Outreach Clinic, something this town definitely needs more of. A brass plaque by the side of the door reads:

Resident Physician: Jerome Llewellyn, MD, NCVS.

Before you ask, yes, we are related. He's my younger brother by a couple of years, and we chose entirely different career paths, though it's not surprising, really. We were — and still are — two different animals. I went into the PD and wore a badge; he took the Oath and wears a white coat. Where I made Dad proud, Jerome made Mom proud. It's kinda been that way since we were pups; any time some bully would pick on him, I'd be there to fight for him, usually get my ass kicked, and he'd be ready with a band-aid and a kind word. I never trust anyone but him with my health concerns, especially since the department-funded doctors got me retired.

I burst in through the wooden doors, my head feeling like it's full of cotton, my vision wobbling and blurring. Wanda is on desk, an aging, sagging rat matriarch that my brother keeps on to deal with the massive amount of paperwork his practice produces. She knows me, and visibly starts, mainly from my abrupt entrance, but also from the amount of blood covering me. It's my own, from the several bleeding cuts on my hand. There's nobody else in the waiting room, so she bustles out, her tail twitching as she goes, probably to find my brother. I feel a strange twist in my stomach. That's not good. I clutch on to the brown paper bag I've been tucking under my arm for about a quarter of a mile like my life depends on it, and I find a seat. I slump down hard. Then the ground rises to meet me, uncushioned, and I know something is terribly, horribly wrong. I barely even register the impact.

Can't fall asleep. If I sleep, I might not wake up again. A delirium drifts into my mind. Can't…

Green…
(what?)
Green and liquid…
(where?)
Green and liquid and warm…
(what's going on?)
Green and liquid and warm and endless…
(this seems kinda nice, actually)
Green and REX!

I open my eyes and there are a bunch of blurring, swirling, crazy green shapes in front of me. I can hear a voice calling for me. It's calling my name, distorted through the haze of absurdity around me, but still there. The blurriness in my vision keeps me from seeing too clearly. I'm on my back and very uncomfortable. When did that happen? My head is pounding like a drum being beaten by a child with a short attention span. As the fog in my eyes gradually clears, I see that it's Jerome standing over me like a guardian angel. Just like old times, eh brother? I try to move, but my body doesn't seem to want to respond, at least not in the way I want it to.

"Rex, are you all right?" comes Jerome's voice, still distorted by the mental fog I'm in, though there's more than a note of worry in it.

"Wha hopp'n?" I slur, the words barely passing my lips.

"Ah… Thank St Roch, you're all right," Jerome sighs. "You had me worried there for a minute."

I feel him fiddling around with something that's stuck in my arm, but I can't physically turn my head to look. My neck isn't obeying me. He's probably got me on a drip. I try to bring my head up, but it flops uselessly with a thud.

"Buh wha happ'n?" The words slither out of me like a slug. Jerome just shakes his head and sighs again.

"You got roofied, Rex," he says matter-of-factly. "You collapsed as soon as Wanda came to find me, or at least that's how it seemed. I know what you're thinking. I smelled the toxins on you, but I've seen and smelled enough junkies and date-rape victims to know that you weren't poisoned. You were drugged."

My mind starts to clear, and my vision has stopped wobbling, at least enough for me to see my brother clearly. I work around the various groups of muscles in my body until I reach my right paw, the one that got gashed, and I hold it where

I can see it. There are bandages on it, clean and sterile as you'd expect of a professional. Good old Jerome. Another band-aid, but a world-wearier word than when we were pups. Nobody ever said the medical profession was easy, especially running a non-profit outreach clinic in Coldwater.

"Thanks, Jer…" I say faintly.

"No problem, Rex. What troubles me is how it happened," Jerome says. "I mean, I picked a whole mess of glass out of your paw, but how it got mixed up with all that venom and all those tranquilizers escapes me. I suppose I shouldn't ask."

He shoots me one of those crooked smiles we always used to exchange as pups, the one that says he knows exactly what's going on, but he'd rather hear it from me personally. I look back to him, my own smile more derelict than crooked, and try to get myself up. I can feel the strength coming back into my body, but it's only gradual, so I go slowly, just enough for me to cope with. I rise carefully, the needle tugging at my right arm, below my rolled-up sleeve. My head spins momentarily, the world going into a vertigo spiral that turns my stomach. I lean unexpectedly, and Jerome catches me before I have the chance to keel over.

"Whatever it was that hit you, it was strong," he says.

"No shit," I reply, about as articulate as I can be at the moment.

"But what *were* you doing?" he asks, genuine concern resonant in his voice. I know I can trust him, both as my doctor and as my brother.

"I came in… package…" I fight to get the words out of my brain. "Still had it? You have it?"

Jerome steadies me into an upright position, and I grip the steel frame of the bed with both hands, just so I don't topple off. Once he's convinced I can sit properly, he crosses to his desk and picks up the bag I'd brought in, depositing it next to me. The dark blood is still crusting on its surface, and it still smells vaguely of venom and pheromones. I shake my head to try and clear my mind, but it just knocks the world off-kilter again.

"Little help here?" I mutter to Jerome, and he takes the hint, emptying the contents of the package onto the table next to me. I look down at what falls out: a tiny black t-shirt and a lime green miniskirt, both size eight and covered in blood, along with a small, brown leather coin-purse, a pair of stiletto heels, and a miniature spray-bottle of artificial dog pheromones. Canis Enfatuum, can you believe. Wherever Ayani went to, she was probably dressed in just her skivvies, but I can understand her needing to get the blood off her. It'd look incriminating. Besides, zebras often have a thing for dressing skimpily in their homelands due to how hot it can get, so modesty certainly wasn't an issue. It's really the purse that intrigues me, though. I delicately pick it up, the strength returning to my hands as the adrenaline builds in my body from the discovery. My battered fingers quiver as I clumsily undo the catch sealing the purse shut.

Most of the contents are pretty mundane; a few receipts, a few dollars in banknotes, a couple of dollars in change, a tampon (equine-sized and unused), a miniature nail-file, a loose cigarette paper or two, and a credit card made out to one Ms Z O Onyelé (Newland Express). Unremarkable, to be sure, but a couple of things definitely stand out. There's a small knag of wood in there, alongside an identity card. My mind tumbles over itself, trying to coordinate my actions. Jerome must have picked up on something, the difficulty I'm still experiencing, as he pulls the I.D. from its resting place. We both stare intently at the card, scrutinizing every detail.

It's an I.D. card from the Zebra Nation. That's to be expected; she is a zebra, after all. The miniscule text is written in several other languages besides Anglish, mainly Caloise, but also a couple of others I don't recognize. This strikes me as a little odd. Most I.D.s and passports are only written in Anglish and Caloise, possibly Caimanisto or Gallano and nothing else, but this has at least a dozen languages on it, from the intricate characters of Kongwu, to the languid, fluid lines of Al-Hayawani. I can't read them, but they're recognizable. There's a picture of Ayani on there, too, certainly much older than the photo Ziva had originally shown me, though I doubt she looks that way now. This thing was issued nearly two years ago. She's dressed tastefully and conservatively, but the look in her eye tells me she's hating every second of it, which adds a bit of weight to my theories about her personality. Hell, Orcowitz's license photo looked positively ecstatic by comparison. Something catches my attention, though. A short line, almost buried under the rest of the miniscule text, reads:

Without Let or Hindrance.

If those words were on a passport, I wouldn't have raised an eyebrow. On an I.D. card, though, that poses a few questions. My body tenses up, and Jerome steadies me, but that could mean a lot of things. The I.D., I mean. The blood rushes to my head, and those weird, green, indescribable shapes invade for a second, knocking me off-balance. I regain my composure, Jerome hanging onto me like a lifeguard, and I shake my head violently to dispel the nonsense and refocus on the card.

"You okay, Rex?" Jerome says to me.

"Yeah," I reply. "Just a few th' afferfex…"

I had meant to say 'a few of the aftereffects', but the words obviously lost their way and decided to have a drink. Jerome says nothing and loosens his grip on me a bit. From an entire life of growing up together, he knows I'm a tough cookie. He gets up and moves to his desk to fetch something. I don't know what. Hopefully, something to help me not feel like shit. My head still feels like it doesn't belong to me, and I'm still slurring a bit, but I manage to engage Jerome from whatever he's doing.

"Thisss is who I'm lookin' for," I say to him, pointing haphazardly at the picture on the I.D. card, the words strangely hissing out of me. "Have you ssseen her?"

"Another one of your cases, Rex?" he replies, testing my eyes with a tiny, bright light, barely skipping a beat. "I thought as much. But no, I haven't seen her. The zebra community is pretty small in Coldwater, other than the streetwalkers I have to deal with. Miserable sorts. Usually come in with something nasty, or, worst case, a foal on the way. Sad, but it's their life. I just hope those foals have a better life than their dams."

"She's not a streetwalker, Jer," I say, the resolution returning to me, as my brother moves the light around to check my reactions. "But she might have come here looking for cheap medical attention. Might have been injured recently."

Jerome returns the light to his desk before walking back to me, and he sits lightly on the edge of the bed, his brow knitting in thought for a moment. I can read my brother like a book. Or at least I think I can.

"Nope, sorry, Rex," he says. "Can't tell you. You know I took the Fitzpatrick Oath. I can't let you know who I see, no matter what it might mean to you, in a professional capacity or otherwise. Doctor-patient confidentiality is sacred. Strictly speaking, I shouldn't even be discussing any of my other patients with you, whatever their life choices."

Just like Jerome; honest to a fault and always upholding the Oath. I sigh heavily and glance down at my paw. It's bandaged up tight, but at least I can move my fingers easily enough. I turn my attention back to the knag of wood in the purse and fumble around trying to fish it out, finally picking it up carefully. There seem to be a few scraps of yellow paint left on it, but I don't understand the significance. Jerome mumbles in recognition beside me.

"A Spirit Key," he says, quietly,

"A what?" I say to him,

"It's a Spirit Key," Jerome repeats, a little louder this time. "It's a Zebra Nation custom that I read about a while ago. When someone of noble birth comes of age, they're given a ceremonial mask, and a single sliver of wood is carved off. Supposedly the owner has to keep it with them at all times to keep evil spirits away. A lot of the superstition seems to have gone from it these days, though. It's more of a rite of passage now, and only members of the minor nobility really believe in the Key's power. At least, that's what I read. It was a good article, too."

My ears twitch as the puzzle pieces start to click together in my mind. Ayani and Ziva are of noble birth, after all. That would also explain the weird I.D. card with a ton of languages on it. The family must travel a lot. They probably have diplomatic immunity... A thought hits me.

"Jerome, do you happen to have a copy of today's paper lying around anywhere?" I ask, the grogginess entirely gone from my body following that revelation,

"Sure," he says, getting up and crossing back to his desk, before picking up a copy of the Herald from a magazine rack. He hands it to me.

"What do you need it for?" He asks, but I ignore the question, busily trying to unscramble the pages and put them back in their correct order. Jerome likes to get to the sports section, just like I do, right after reading the comic strips, but a bad habit of his is that he always pulls the pages out of order. I stand up somehow, the I.V. tugging at my arm painfully, but I don't care. I remember seeing something earlier today in the headlines, so I spread the pages on the bed, scanning them as I go. Jerome looks on, dumbfounded at what I'm doing, but he soon starts wordlessly helping me to spread the news sheets out. I'll know what it is I'm looking for when I see it, and soon enough, it's there in front of me.

The headline reads: Ambassador's Reception Wows Socialites, Diplomatic Ties Stronger than Ever.

It seems innocuous enough, but I start to read further into the article than I had this morning, given what I've just found out. A lot of the spread is made up of photographs and the usual sniping comments about some celebrity wife's outfit or other, but the pertinent information has to be buried in here somewhere. Let's see... attendees... the Mayor of Oldsburg, the diplomatic attaché from the Capitol, a few celebrities from Tinseltown... Sanford Lynns is standing out among the names mentioned, the father of one of the dead cats from the fight, though there's no picture of him. As I'm scanning the article, nothing really sticks out until I start re-reading it. Then it hits me right between the eyes worse than the Mickie Finn I'd accidentally been stricken with. How could I have missed it?

"Guests were treated to a gala evening to greet the visiting

Zebra Nation ambassador, Otongye Onyelé." It reads, "Although the ambassador himself was unable to attend, due to urgent business in the Capitol, his daughter, Ms Ziva Onyelé, made a most gracious appearance and shook hands with Mayor Stahl on behalf of her father and her Nation."

I feel like the world should have just ground to a halt, but the momentum is too great. Ziva and Ayani are the daughters of the Zebra Nation ambassador. I should have guessed before now, really, but I'm not especially up on my international politics. I draw my eyes back to just below the headline to see who wrote the article, and another piece falls into place. Jennifer Cassidy. I feel almost foolish for not picking up on that. It's her style. She must have charmed her way into a temporary freelance position at the Herald. It makes sense, too, as much as I hate to admit it. She used to work for them years ago, back when she was a cub reporter, and working for Ziva would give almost unlimited access to any bits of information she — or the editors — might want. That could be why she's back in Oldsburg. I need to know, but as I am right now, I might need my brother to keep me upright.

I turn to Jerome, the adrenaline wearing off, his stony, inscrutable face looking back at me. That's something he always had a talent for; he always had — and has — a face that seems indifferent to whatever nonsense I'm getting up to. I smirk, knowing that I've found what I need. But the needle is still in my arm, and the gentle pull of it is starting to get on my nerves. Jerome picks up on this.

"You want that out, Rex?" He asks, though he doesn't sound too ready to let me out on my own. I simply nod.

"You'll have to leave that bandage on for a couple of days," he says, taking my arm. "Then have those stitches out in about a week. Come back once that's done; I'll need to check on it. Try not to do too much with that hand, okay?"

I nod again before a very fundamental question invades my thoughts.

"How long have I been here?" I ask,

"You came in about a quarter past two," says Jerome. "And, by my watch, it's near enough half seven."

My insides jump as he says this. Have I really wasted nearly half a day? The green reverie really took up that long? Needless to say, I take a seat and let him take the drip out, me clutching a cotton ball in the crook of my arm. I still feel a little bit woozy, but I have more leads to work on and a few bits of physical evidence to show to Ziva, though how I'm going to get into the Zebra Nation Embassy is another matter. Then again, if Jen can do it, so can I. We're both on Ziva's payroll after all, or at least it's safe to assume that. I straighten myself up, roll my sleeve back down, and grab my coat and hat. My left ear twitches as I place the felt fedora on my head, as it always does. It's strange how you never notice these things in normal life. Must be the adrenaline sharpening my awareness of all those little things my body does that I never consciously notice. At least Jerome has put all the evidence in a sterilized bag for me to take back to the office. I wrap it in a sheet of newspaper so as not to arouse too much suspicion. My brother then turns to me, a serious look on his face.

"Rex, whatever is going on, you need to take care of yourself," he says.

"I know," I reply half-heartedly.

"I'm not just saying this as your doctor, you know?" He says, genuine concern in his voice. "I'm saying this as your brother who loves you. You could be messing with forces beyond your control, and I don't want to see you hurt… or worse."

"I know, Jer," I say, not unkindly, turning for the door to leave. "But we both know the risks of my line of work."

"We both knew the risks when you were with the PD," retorts Jerome. "But you don't have the department backing you up now. You're just a civilian with a license. The fact that you're carrying that old pistol around with you is proof enough that something's got you rattled. Did you think I wouldn't notice?"

I feel the pressure of the holster at my side become suddenly uncomfortable. Damn. Jerome always could tell when something was up. Serves me right for walking around armed, too, I guess.

"It almost destroyed dad when you were retired from the force," he says, somberly. "Have you ever thought about what it might do to him if you got shot? Or killed? Is this really worth it?"

I don't turn back to Jerome. I simply stare into the middle distance, squarely at the door, the cheap woodgrain staring back, formulating my response for maximum impact. I can't let this get to me, can't make Jerome worry. He'd know.

"To a sister missing her sibling, to a girl frightened for her life, to a guy who lost his brother, to a father who lost a son… Yeah, I'd say it's worth it," I finally say, every word calculated. "And I'll get to the bottom of this case if I have to go through hell and back to do it."

As I open the door to leave, bag under my arm, I hear Jerome slump heavily into his chair, defeated. I don't turn back. I can't relent. I have to be firm in my convictions. As I close the door, with the sterile corridors of the clinic echoing around me, my acute hearing picks up a single whispered sentence from Jerome. It's something I don't want to hear, and my heart sinks in my chest.

"That's what I was afraid of…" he says.

The sun is already setting over Oldsburg as I make my way home, casting the city in twilight shades of purple, grey, and blue, wrestling for dominance against the sickly yellow glow of the thousands of streetlights that line every road. The ever-present rumble of traffic and honking horns murmurs in the distance, a constant companion wherever one goes in the city, punctuated by the occasional siren of a squad car or ambulance. There are some folk who say they can't sleep without city noises in the background, and I'd be inclined to believe them. It's like the city's own personal lullaby, as haunting and tumultuous as it may be.

In the distance, rising above the rooftops and peering between the skyscrapers and chimney-stacks, stands the Statue of Harmony, right at the mouth of the Holbrook River. The statue itself is of an elegant bronze nanny goat in a robe and crown, carrying a book and holding up an orb of fire, her face stern yet motherly. She's meant to be a symbol of peace and hope among all animals, though I think if she could see the state of her city right now, she'd probably get off her pedestal and walk away with tears in her eyes, never to be seen again. That'd never happen, though. It's physically impossible, for one thing. I wonder how many boatloads of immigrants had witnessed the unblinking stare of Mother Harmony upon arriving in Oldsburg? I bet my grandpa did, back in his day.

I decide to go only as far as I need in order to get on the subway. My apartment is at the northern end of the Bowery, and I don't really have it in me to hike all that distance today, not right now. Coldwater doesn't have a station within its boundaries, but I hear Mayor Stahl is trying to push through some contract or other to extend the line. Yeah, *that'll* be the day. The nearest stop I know of is in the neighboring borough of the Hollows. It's bat country, not quite as dangerous as Coldwater, but definitely not someplace you'd want to be after dark. Bats are very clannish, and their neighborhood 'vigilance committees' can be just as blood-hungry as any pack, though they always claim it's just for the defense of their colonies. The unwritten rule is that if you stay out of their way, they'll stay out of your way, but don't count on it. I'm just thankful for the ordinance that prohibits vampire bats from taking up residence within the city limits due to their dietary requirements. All the blood banks and slaughterhouses in the city couldn't cope with the kind of pressure even a single colony could apply.

I manage to get myself to the subway station that serves this end of the Hollows and buy a ticket. It's a good thing I have enough for the train fare, but I still fumble with the bills as I clutch the package under my weaker arm. Having a messed-up paw is a lot more trouble than you'd expect. I ignore the strange look from the pigeon cashier and make my way through the turnstile to the platform. Every step of the way, the walls are covered with graffiti of varying quality and meaning, from simple, crude scrawls to paintwork of almost mural quality. I spot a couple of gang signs among the jumble of spray paint and markers, a vague recollection from my days on the force, mainly from various committees that I'd dealt with. Looks like this is part of the Leatherwing Krew's turf. I really hope I don't run into any of them.

The station is quiet, the stale, musty gusts of air echoing

through the tunnels and the rumble of distant engines the only sounds to hear. The smell of stale piss pervades everywhere, nearly crushed beneath the scents of oil and dead air, but still there. Even the constant white noise of the traffic above doesn't penetrate this far underground. I sit on one of the steel benches by the track and wait. I notice that I'm not alone, as there's a hobo, bundled up so well I can't tell what species he (or she?) is, snoring softly in a corner nearby. I can smell him or her from here, though, as a half-empty bottle of Old Seadog rum lies at their side, loosely clutched in fingers blistered by poverty. They'll probably get back to drinking it when they wake up, if only to fight off the hangover and the horrid, crushing reality of being homeless. I shake my head and smile sourly to myself. I could be there myself, given a bad week. Man, I could use a drink and a smoke when I get home, especially after the day I've had. The train pulls into the station, and I stand, my knees clicking quietly, and step aboard.

The carriage smells just as awful, reeking of fast-food, urine, and body odor. It wears a dog down, all these terrible smells. I've been in nightclub bathrooms that smelled more pleasant. The look and feel of the car itself are just as bad, with sticky floors, flickering lights overhead, graffiti on the windows, and more than a few damp seats. I sniff around a bit and find one bench that's relatively dry, and sit myself uncomfortably in it. There's not another soul on the train, though, and that helps put me at ease. Needless to say, the ride home should give me a few minutes of respite to collect my thoughts and arrange my notes. My bandaged hand roots around in my pocket like it's not my own, and I bring out my cheap notepad, flicking through what I know already. I might have to write left-handed with my stubby pencil on a constantly swaying subway train, but I need to get everything down on paper before I forget any of it. I just really hope I can read it later.

From the newspaper article, the multilingual I.D. card, and the Spirit Key that Jerome enlightened me about, my initial suspicions about Ayani and Ziva's status as wealthy zebras were correct, but I had no idea they were connected to anything political. Their father is the Zebra Nation ambassador, which explains why Pettibone wanted me to conduct this case on the quiet. The discarded clothes and purse also indicate that Ayani didn't want to be identified on the night of the fight at the Watering Hole, but she couldn't have gone too far without being noticed unless she had someone to get her away from the scene quickly. Something about that doesn't add up, but I'm not sure what. Could she really have had someone pick her up that fast? If so, who? It's conjecture, sure, but it's a possibility.

Also on my mind is the fact that Jen is probably involved more deeply with the Onyelé family than I had initially thought. I need to get in touch with her and find out what she knows, though I have to be subtle about it. I can probably reach her at the Herald, or at least someone who can give me her details while she's in town. As much as I hate to admit it, given our history, I need that lady, though I sincerely wish that I didn't.

There are only a couple more stops until Horner Park, the station closest to where I live in the Bowery. The carriage sways into a shallow left turn, the overhead lights blinking out fleetingly with the train's movement. I manage to shove the notebook and pencil awkwardly into my pocket, a brief, slightly numb sensation coursing through the tips of my bandaged fingers before the feeling comes back just as quickly. For some reason, I test the weight of the package I've been hanging on to since leaving Jerome. I don't know why. Maybe it just feels oddly reassuring to have some substantial physical evidence to show for all the trouble I've been through lately. Before I know it, the train screeches to a halt at Horner Park, and the doors of the car rattle open stiffly. I rise, equally stiffly, and exit the train, making my way above ground, ready to head home. I've got a lot of planning to do for the days ahead.

Eduardo is having another one of his damned parties again. At least the music doesn't tip the Richter scale this time around. I manage to wrestle the keys from my coat pocket with my messed-up paw and get myself inside, though the hubbub of conversation and laughter from upstairs makes me wish I'd stayed outside. That all fades into nonexistence, though, as I grab a cigarette from the pack I'd left on my desk. I touch the paper tube to my lips and strike the flint of my lighter, the fire springing up brighter than the flames of Mother Harmony. The subtle crackling of the fire taking to the cigarette, followed by the hit of the smoke. By St Roch, that's something worth living for, even though I know it's going to eventually shorten my lifespan. As for right now, though, I don't care. Given the trippy ride I've been through, little of which I really got to experience or remember, I feel I deserve this smoke. In the dim, flickering light of my apartment — my office space and general redoubt from the world — the sinuous shapes that rise from the end of my cigarette suggest a totally different world. Could I be part of that world beyond mortal constraints and boundaries? What am I saying? No chance... I need to get over the nonsense in my mind that still lingers.

I shake my head vigorously, trying to dispel the cobwebs and absurd thoughts that dwell there. I need to concentrate on what is important to the case. Still... my eyes are drooping. Don't know if it's my lifestyle or the roofies that's hitting me harder right now. Damn, Jerome said those things were strong. Can't really fall asleep right now, but...

Boscoe. I remember his grizzly face, smiling one moment like a brother, serious as a mortician the next. He taught me a lot back in those days. The shot, that one fateful bullet. Why? What happened with that? I always thought that something leaked out about the cops doing some misdemeanor. Was it true? The sound-proof cells immediately caught my mind. The Oldsburg system can't work, I think to myself, like some fluid reasoning that I can't explain. It was a call that we had responded to, just a couple of guys in uniform. Something happened. A bad bust. Violence, dust, and eventually death.

Are any of us really innocent? Was it really my fault?

I awaken abruptly in my office, sitting bolt upright, my tongue dry from where it had been lolling out of my open mouth. Haven't done that since I was a pup. My face doesn't exactly feel great either. I must have just passed out on my desk, I reason, as I pick a few biscuit crumbs out of the fur on my cheek, feeling the numbness dissipate from where I'd been lying. The cigarette, still between my fingers, has long since burned to a thin line of ash. I glance at the clock on the opposite wall. It's just after ten, so I figure that I haven't been out for that long, maybe a couple of hours. The low thrum of music can still be heard above me, though it's a lot less lively.

I scan around my desk, looking for a bottle, and pick up the last dregs of the one I'd bought a couple of days before. I don't even bother with a glass, just unscrewing the top and gulping down the last, fiery gulps of the whiskey. The sensation runs through me like a lightning bolt, and I wince through the hit of the alcohol. I really need to cut down, but not right now, not today. I say that to myself all the time, but I never listen to myself. I guess that's why I can never really quit drinking. I just can't say no to myself, no matter how hard I try.

I need to pick up on a couple more leads on this case. The fight at the Watering Hole stills seems like it could have a bearing on the case, and I know that Daniel Arden had had some sort of threats against his safety, at least from what Benny Orcowitz had told me. There might be a link with Ayani, but I can't quite put a finger on the how or the why. The educational campus at the university will be closed right now, but I'd bet the farm that the student union bars will be swinging until well into the morning, especially on a Friday night. How reliable the students might be is in question, though. They like to blow off steam as much as anybody, and I'm sure that by the time I've reached U of O, across the Holbrook, they'll probably be as steamed as a Scotia crab. Still, I need some background details about Danny Arden and what he was going through. It could have some bearing. He can't have kept all of his problems to himself. There must be someone that he confided in, possibly the other members of the university basketball team. Although I know two of those members are dead, that leaves at least two still kicking on the main team, plus the subs bench, which constitutes, in total, another seven animals. Maybe they're out on the town tonight? I damn well hope so.

I guess that's made my mind up, at least as far as that line of inquiry goes. I need to get in with the young crowd, St Roch help me. I search through my wardrobe for the youngest-looking and most fashionable things I can find. I'm out of luck. The best I can find is an old pinstripe waistcoat and pants in navy blue, the jacket long ago eaten by moths in all the wrong places. Well, I might either turn up looking dapper as all sin or become a laughing-stock, but I change just the same, my right paw aching with each movement. That'd look weird, though not much weirder than a Corgi in his middling years trying to fit in with animals less than half his age. But then again, the Tinseltown and Goldgate guys come over to Oldsburg looking for new starlets or possible wives... or at least an easy screw, masquerading as one or the other. I wouldn't look so unusual among those lounge lizards, reptilian or not.

Once I've clumsily pulled on my garments and combed the loose crumbs from my face, I feel a little better equipped to meet the student scene, especially since the whole ensemble looks kind of slimming on me. I leave my piece and my stunner at home. I know I won't need them. These kids have nothing on me, and the packs and vigilance committees tend to steer clear of the university, at least so far as open activity is concerned. I even have a quick shave. It's amazing what an electric razor can do for a guy my age. I call up Sid, he picks me up, and we're on our way into the urban wilderness.

It's past eleven by the time Sid and I roll up outside the student union bars near the University. Sid didn't really know the way, and going across the river really screwed both of us up, directionally speaking. He tends to work the East side, and I haven't really been across the Holbrook in a good while.

113

Eventually, though, we muddled our way through it. He didn't even charge me for the wrong turns; we respect each other that much, even though I'm sure his boss at the cab company is going to chew him out for being short. I pay him what I owe him, which is still pretty steep for the distance, but I know Sid would never knowingly overcharge me. I stand for a second to get my bearings and take in the local scenery, reaching into my pocket for a cigarette.

I feel like a stranger in a foreign land, a land that I never even experienced when I was younger. I went pretty much straight from school into the Police Academy, just like my dad did, so this is all alien to me. I thought the strip clubs and dive bars in Coldwater were flashy with their neons, but just one of these student joints could give a whole football field's worth of Christmas trees a run for their money. The night is already alive, jumping to the sounds of the latest bands, with students of all species stumbling their way from one bar to the next, or else crouching down outside to have a smoke behind a dumpster, somewhere they won't be seen in the highly improbable scenario that their parents just happen to come cruising by. I guess they don't want to put their trust funds in danger. Young people never really change, no matter how old you get. I might even have pulled in an older sibling of theirs when I was on the force, possibly even on a night just like this, to cool their heels in the drunk tank.

The sleaze is already crawling amongst these kids, too, the older males with cash to burn and desires to be sated. I spot more than a few groups of girls forming an entourage around some wealthy-looking type. A gecko, not dressed too dissimilarly to myself, casually strolls past, a dame on each arm, one a cat, the other a vixen, both cooing over their sugar-

114

daddy. Looks like I might need some arm-candy if I'm going to be taken seriously around here, but good luck finding any girl who'll be seen in the company of an overweight, over-aged corgi with outdated fashion sense like yours truly. I check the watch on my right wrist. It's already coming up to a quarter past eleven. I scratch my chin with my good hand, contemplating what I should do, the cigarette dangling unlit from my lips.

It's at this point that a familiar face, or should I say, a familiar body comes into view. I can tell because that particular figure was rubbing against me the other night at the Watering Hole. It's that Ramona girl, the raccoon, though you couldn't tell given her current attire. She's dressed pretty dowdy, with thick, studious glasses on her muzzle, her curves stuffed uncomfortably into a U of O sweater that's at least one size too small for her. Her chubby thighs are hidden by a billowing maxi skirt, but it does absolutely nothing to hide her muffin-top. The only other real indications of her femininity are the bobby-socks she's showing above a pair of worn but serviceable saddle shoes, scuffed white patent leather on black. She's clutching a stack of papers and books to her ample chest, mainly concerning journalism and publishing law, judging by the titles. Must have been at the library until closing time. I guess she's really serious about her degree. I'm not sure if I should wave or not, but I don't need to be. She notices my ugly mug in the crowd and makes a bee-line for me, completely oblivious to the drunken revelers around her.

"Hi!" she says breathlessly. "You're the guy I saw the other night, right? The reporter?"

Crap. I suddenly remember the bullshit story I gave to her, and I decide to play along. Couldn't really hurt, right?

"Yeah," I say cordially. "Rex Llewellyn. I saw you too. Ramona, right? Still keeping at the ol' grindstone, huh?"

I casually nod towards the books she's carrying. She flusters for a second, giggling lightly but eventually regaining her composure.

"Y-yeah," she stammers, breathless again. "It's all go, y'know? Can't let it drop for a second!"

She shoots me a grin that's wider than her face, and I'm pretty sure it's what knocks a few books out of her hands. I react, but she reacts too, and by the time we're done being reactionary, most of her class notes and books are spread across the sidewalk like fallen leaves. The other students pay no mind, just on their way to the next cheap beer or shot. Some even blindly step through the scattered papers, heedless of the two animals picking them up, only drunkenly turning back to offer a half-hearted apology. Ramona and I scramble around as best we can to grab the scraps of loose paper swirling around in the breeze and on the pavement. She's pretty grateful once we're done, her breath returning to her.

"So, what brings you here tonight, Mr. Llewellyn? More to do with the Watering Hole case?" she asks,

"No, no… following a slightly different lead," I say to her. "I'm looking more into Danny Arden's social life."

Her expression changes from fangirlish familiarity to suspicion. Did I say something wrong?

"How come you call him Danny?" she asks, a hardness coming into her voice. "Nobody at the university called him Danny, not even the coach. I don't even think Mary Lansing called him Danny, and she was his girlfriend."

I'm foundering here. She's sharp, much sharper than I'd originally imagined. Can't let her know the real details of the case, though. I gather my response into a smug ball and try to hit a strike-out with it. Guess I must be pitching bad because she hits it like a line drive.

"Yeah, the, uh… Arden Shipping Corporation wanted me to find out a bit more than what the police could tell them," I lie. She's not buying it, not any more.

"You're not a reporter at all, are you?" she hisses, closing in on me. "What are you really after?"

I guess I need to come clean with her. I knew that the flimsy pretense of being a journalist had to be brought down some time, especially to a journalism major. I sigh and flop my hands to my sides, the bandaged one twitching in pain. I'm only thankful that Ramona hadn't noticed it before and still hasn't. I don't quite know if I can trust her with the information I have, but it might help to have a fresh pair of eyes on things, and a sharp pair at that.

"I'm a private detective," I say to her, frankly. "I'm working a case that may have to do with Daniel Arden's killing, only I don't quite know how. There are a lot of things that link up, but it still makes no sense."

Ramona's expression softens a bit, now that she knows the truth (at least what I'm willing to tell her), but she still has a stony look in her eye. I guess she's not used to people lying to her. To my surprise, she draws even closer to me, those full hips pushing uncomfortably against me, her lips brushing my ear.

"What will it take to find out?" she asks, curling her mouth into a smile like a spider beckoning a fly. She's not that evil, is she? I figure not. She seems too much of a good girl for that. Then again, good girls are only bad girls that don't get caught. Is she trying to hint that she can help me?

"I just need a date for the union bars," I say, my own mouth drying with every word. "Just to keep up the image of an out-of-towner."

"You've found one, Mr. Llewellyn," she says coyly. With the flick of a finger and an unspoken word, she leads me through the campus grounds back to her place, a dorm just off-site. I follow dumbly, not wanting to lose that thread of investigation. It's a four-story brick building, pristinely kept, and I'm asked to wait at the door by a couple of ox doormen, big bruisers, but nowhere near the size of Bill, while Ramona scurries inside. Two cigarettes and a few minutes later, she reappears, not in the slutty attire I'd seen on her at the club, and not in the frumpy clothes I'd seen her in just a few minutes ago, but in something that I guess sort of falls in-between. I think you might call it party-wear. Alluring yet modest. Tasteful yet raunchy. Red sequins around the shoulders, complementing her deep brown fur. Stiletto heels in the same devilish red. I can't tell from looking, but she seems to have slimmed, possibly a girdle.

I shake my head at the attempted gorgeousness that is this raccoon coming down the stairs, who had only days ago been just another stripper with nothing but a name and a connection. I mean, she looks great, but she's less than half my age. Then again, that's just what I'm looking for right now, if only to keep up appearances. She links arms with me, and we're on our way. We chat the case a little as we go, as far as Danny is concerned, but I leave Ayani's name out of it. Can't give the whole game away on a pop fly.

The music is so loud I can barely hear myself think. The thudding of the bassline is almost hurting my soul, though it syncs up pretty well with the march of eternity and the beating of the hundreds of hearts already on the dancefloor. I'm hot and bothered, my tongue lolling as I pant for breath, having already experienced two dances with Ramona. And yes, 'experienced' is the right word. I need a time-out. She'd dragged me off to one of the busiest student clubs imaginable. I can't even remember what it's called, and I'm far too old for this shit, though I have to give Ramona credit for getting me past the door.

I compose myself for a moment at the bar. The greyhound behind the counter asks me my order, but it's drowned out by the music. I can barely see her past the crush of bodies, but I can definitely make out fake lashes and gaudily manicured nails. By my guess, the rest is probably just as trashy. I do catch the painted lips, though, so I order as best I can through gestures and mouth-shapes. Just a beer. She seems to get the gist and hurries off to fetch my order. Even the Watering Hole wasn't this loud, but, philosophically, I can see the appeal. As a young adult, regardless of species, nobody understands you, so why hear them — or anything — at all? Big whoop, teenage angst and all that jazz. In fairness, I'd rather be listening to jazz than whatever electronic monstrosity is currently playing, but that's just me, it seems.

Ramona has somehow managed to muscle her way through the crowd back to me, though, given her frame, that's not surprising. She's missing a few sequins, and my guess is they're either on someone's jacket or on the dancefloor. She has a slightly smug look on her face, and I scan my eyes around at the prissy cat girls watching her from the dark corners of the bar. There's a hint of jealousy in their eyes, and the student politics suddenly come sharply into focus. Seems Ramona isn't well-liked amongst the female students, or at least doesn't command much respect normally. Seems hanging around me has caused a stir. She leans heavily on the bar, and I can barely hear her over the riot of sound around us. My dog hearing makes up for a lot of it, though, for which I'm very thankful.

"Seen anything?" she shouts above the racket.

"Not yet," I bellow back to her. I lean in close to her, close enough to smell the Montrose No. 7 perfume that she wears like a badge of honor, and decide to shout into her tufty, pointed ear to at least try and be heard.

"I need people who knew Daniel Arden," I shout, hoping that she understood the words. The strobe lights flash as she pulls me closer.

"Was that Daniel Arden?" she screams back to me over the din. I simply nod, and she takes the hint, her little, dark eyes sparkling in the flashing, jumping strobe lights around us. I'm not hoping to gain much here. It was probably a bad idea to do this, anyway. Most of the students here are already stinking drunk, more concerned with trying to get laid or at least dance away their cares. I've already tried to ask the bar staff what they know, but none of them are in a talkative mood, which is understandable. There's always another rowdy further down, that needs attending to, and why should they care about a pointless question?

A random beer finds its way to my hand, but I still have my eyes on Ramona, or at least her approximate position. She seems to be looking for someone, or possibly a list of several people that she knows. She's not too subtle about it, either. I can see the gap in the dancefloor where she moves. The pure, unadulterated tide of student bodies just sort of swallows her up and spits her out at random, the strange hole amongst them reforming around her a few seconds later. The clamorous, thundering beat still hurts my ears. I idly sip at the beer that's already warming up to room temperature in my hand, the tangy bubbles refreshing my senses a bit while also tasting absolutely foul. Ugh. It's that craft junk that's all the rage these days. I notice the server at my elbow prodding me, and I absent-mindedly slip her a bill for the drink, but my attention stays firmly fixed on where Ramona could be. I don't even notice until much later in the evening that the server never even gave me any change. Either craft beer is as expensive as I thought it could be, or the staff are a bunch of thieves. Both options remain a mystery.

I notice the hole pushing its way back to the bar, and Ramona slumps down next to me, almost like she'd been disgorged from the pulsating mass of animality, immediately snatching the beer from my hand and taking a deep swig of it to refresh herself. More of her sequins are missing. She hands back what was once a mostly full plastic cup, now half-gone. I look surprised, and she looks disappointed. She leans in close to me to catch my ear, and her boobs are pressing uncomfortably up against me. Given how big they are, it's not surprising.

"She's not here!" she hollers, the syllables slow and loud, "We need to go somewhere else!"

Somewhere else? Who in St. Roch's name was she looking for? I put the disposable plastic cup down containing my beer, only to have it snatched up by some unknown hand. Seems minesweeping is still a custom among the poor student population. That's the way you have to think with students, like they're a lost tribe, just being discovered by the world. Their ways are not necessarily your ways, and in the sweltering, beating heart of the jungle that is Oldsburg's nightlife, you've got to be prepared for whoever might want you on the dinner menu, whatever that might entail.

Anyway, I feel her tugging my shirt-sleeve, and a twinge of discomfort shoots through my fingers. She leads me away from the dancefloor and outside, pushing past countless bodies and giving a cheery smile to anyone who recognizes her. The majority of them smile back, and I get the feeling she's not so much a social pariah as just a nice person. Petty people hate that. I'm almost surprised at how well she can blend into any crowd she's in. We pass the bouncer, a burly elephant, his wrinkly grey skin covered in tattoos and his ivory adorned with intricate carvings, and he nods us out. The cool air and traffic smell of the street seems almost nectar-sweet compared to the musk of so much melancholy and desperate energy. I immediately reach into my pocket for a smoke, not even caring that my mouth is desert-dry after the crappy beer. Ramona pauses for a moment to let me light up, and she finally notices my hand as I cup the lighter against the wind.

"What happened to you?" she asks. She sounds genuinely shocked.

"Cut myself," I reply, in a slightly snarky manner. "Shaving."

She gets the hint that I'm not going to open up about it. She's a smart kid. It'll take her places. She puts a dainty hand on her thick hip and narrows her eyes before speaking, as though she's searching her memory for something.

"We've got places to be," Ramona says, in a matter-of-fact kind of way. "If she's not here at Standout, she might be at Heartbeats. It's not as much of a dive there, but she occasionally slums it here, y'know?"

"Who?" I ask, confounded by who she's talking about.

"Who else?" she says. "Daniel's girlfriend... or, well... y'know..."

Now I remember. Ramona had let slip that Danny had a girlfriend during our little tête-á-tête at the Watering Hole, and she mentioned her name earlier tonight, Mary Lansing. If he'd confide in anybody, it'd probably be his girlfriend. Ramona links arms with me again, a little more gingerly than the last time, now that she's seen how messed up my paw is, and we head out into the night. I secretly smile to myself as a few heads turn as we pass by. I guess I've still got it after all.

It's two hours later, and two hours drunker, when we finally catch up with Mary Lansing, the girlfriend of the late Daniel Arden. Heartbeats was a total bust, but it didn't stop Ramona or me slugging back a couple of drinks. This pattern continued through the next few bars and clubs; Testament followed Heartbeats, which was followed by Electric City, followed by Rainbows, each club getting fancier than the one before it. If I didn't know any better, I'd swear Ramona was using this as an excuse to go out drinking. Though I'm feeling a bit light-headed and tangling my footing every now and again, Ramona has been clinging on to me like her life depended on it since we left Testament. I'm not sure if that's because she can't hold her drink, or if she just wants to get into my pants. It's not important. We manage to find Mary at The Unity Club, a jazz bar that I'm not unfamiliar with. The moose bouncer checks our I.D.s and lets us into the main room once I've convinced him with a fast fiver.

The lighting is low, the soft sounds of saxophones and muted trumpets deepening the mood, accompanied by the rhythmic brushstrokes of the drummer amid the hazy, dreamlike atmosphere. The big band on stage is playing it slow and sensual, yet melancholy, like they knew the meaning of our arrival; a sad tune heralding sad news for a sad meeting. The audience is sat in rapt fascination, or else talking inaudibly quietly among themselves, so as not to disturb the performance. A few pairs of animals are still shuffling a slow-dance, oblivious to the world. It's late into the night, and you've got to be a real fan of the blues to be sticking around this place at such an hour.

Mary Lansing is sitting by herself at a side table, just away from the main floor, her features chiseled and handsome as a cat should be. She has red rings around her eyes from crying, and it's obvious she's had tears rolling down her cheeks, each one leaving a deep scar of moisture in the lustrous hairs on her face. Ramona had picked her out instantly, despite being in a tipsy state. She's not a bad-looking cat, to be fair. Short and slender, with a mottled, tortoise-shell pattern to her fur that plays wonderfully against the soft light and the smoke in the air. Well-dressed, too: all designer fashion, though nothing too expensive. She's nursing a glass of milk like it's the only thing keeping her last fiber of sanity from snapping.

We approach cautiously, Ramona occasionally stumbling on those dumb heels she decided to wear tonight, and we're virtually on top of poor Mary before she even acknowledges our presence. When she does, she recoils with a start, but not enough to elicit a noise. She just looks ragged and forlorn, without joy or laughter, exhausted by the world.

"What do you want, Marsh?" Mary asks, a cutting edge of hostility in her voice as she recognizes Ramona. "Come to show off your new boyfriend, now that you've finally found one? You realize how gauche that is, given how things have been lately?"

Ramona's grip on my arm suddenly tightens, like she's ready to strangle. It's not good to antagonize a drunk, so I butt in to save us all from a scene.

"Mary Lansing?" I inquire, ignoring Ramona's tiny claws digging into my arm like needles. "The name's Rex Llewellyn. I'm looking into Daniel's murder."

My words fall on deaf ears, Mary's eye fixed firmly on the stage. She takes a long, slow draught of the milk in her hand before answering.

"You and every two-bit paper-boy in town," she finally says. "Once you get a whiff that I was the girlfriend of the late-great-Son-of-Conroy, I can't have a peaceful moment to myself..."

I take a sniff. Yeah, she's been hitting it hard tonight, milk mostly, but there's more than a few vodkas and other alcoholic drinks mixed in amongst it that I can't quite identify. But her expression has softened, and that leads me to believe she's through with fighting it. I pet Ramona's shoulder gently to make her lay off with the claws. She looks up at me with muzzy eyes, a glint of acknowledgment flashing through, and her grip loosens enough for me to breathe a sigh of relief. I could do without needing any more medical attention for a while.

"Mind if we take a seat?" I ask of Mary.

"Might as well," she replies morosely. "Everyone else does when they're not invited..."

Ramona and I sit ourselves on two of the plush, armless chairs that surround the small table, and Mary slumps forward, resting her chin in her hands, a dejected, sad look that instantly tugs at the heartstrings. Her gaze doesn't even deviate from the band on stage.

"So, what is it you want to know?" Mary asks, not even looking at her new guests. "Sex scandals? Doing drugs? I'll give you the same answer as all the others: nothing happened."

"You've got me wrong, Miss Lansing," I begin. "I'm a private detective and…"

"So you're a shamus," she rebuts into my sentence. "Same deal. I'm not saying anything about our relationship."

"Listen," I say, getting more irritated by the minute. "I'm looking into who killed Danny. If you don't want to talk, that's fine, but I think I can help you clear your head of a few things."

The uneasy silence is broken only by the mellow music from onstage, and the soft gurgling coming from Ramona as she tilts back and forth, her arm raised trying to attract a server. The last few couples are still dancing like they're the walking dead, a slow swaying that betrays just how drunk and tired they are. My eyes are kept glued to Mary, or at least her profile, looking for any indication of what she's thinking. Her eyes close slowly, and another moist scar trickles its way through her fur. She opens her eyes and finally turns to us, sniffing heavily.

"Okay…" she says, the words soft and pained. "I'll talk to you. You called him Danny. I thought I was the only one who called him Danny…"

I hate it when dames cry. I grab a couple of disposable napkins from the table and hand them to Mary, only to notice several more screwed-up wads of paper on the floor around her chair. She's been here a while, and with just as much on her mind, I'd figure. Ramona is still trying to catch the attention of a waiter, and I leave her to it. I turn on the soulful eyes and start my questioning.

"Let's start from the beginning," I say calmly and quietly. "Nothing about your relationship. That's not my business. I need to know a few things about Danny, if he had any troubles on his mind or anything like that. Did he tell you anything?"

Mary sniffles into the paper napkin before answering, her breathing rattling, wracked with her own tormenting emotions. This must be painful for her, but it might shed some light on the events leading up to Danny's death.

"I was the last person to see him alive, you know?" she finally says, "We'd had a stupid fight about Danny's dad. About how I thought he probably thought I'd never be good enough for his son. My family isn't super-rich like the Ardens. They're in book publishing, but not like managerial or anything. I'd had these stupid ideas about Conroy, and Danny didn't like it…"

I lean back, taking in those words. Doesn't seem like the picture of romantic bliss, but all couples have stupid arguments that they later regret and make up over, especially about families. I guess Mary will never know that sense of regret, at least not with Daniel Arden. Anyway, I keep asking the questions.

"Did Danny have any enemies?" I ask sincerely. "Anybody that might have wished ill of him? Maybe wanted to hurt him?"

Mary answers in the negative, then goes back to snorting and sniffling into her napkin. By this time, Ramona has managed to flag down a waiter. Mary, very graciously and despite her tears, offers to get us all a drink. Soon enough, the busboy is on his way, fetching a bottle of fine wine. We all sit in relative silence until the booze is brought to our table, along with three glasses. The wine is poured out. A large swig from her glass seems to calm Mary down, her nerves and emotions melting away, though I question the wisdom of taking that much drink in one gulp. I can already see the glazed look in her eye as she steadies herself. The band plays on, the last couple having already vacated the dancefloor.

"Other than the boys from Delta Lambda, no, he didn't have any enemies," Mary slurs out unsteadily, returning to what I just asked. Seems the wine is hitting her hardest of all. "But tha's jus' ol' college ribbing. They wouldn't kill him. He wuz great, yeh…?"

I sip tentatively at my own glass. It's not my drink of choice, so I can't really comment on its quality, but I'm not paying for it, so why complain?

"Not necessarily people on campus," I say to Mary. "Somebody who might have a vendetta against Danny's family. Have you seen anyone hanging around campus that you didn't recognize?"

"Tons of people ev'ry day," she says back. "My social circle's pretty small. No… not small… Elite, that's us…"

"I mean anyone you could say really didn't belong," I reply, sipping at the wine again. Ramona has already finished her glass and is going back for another. Mary thinks for a moment, the rim of her wineglass pressed against her lips, her whiskers stiffening visibly. Seems I've touched on something with that line of inquiry, which is just what I want. I need to keep up this momentum but not go too hard. This girl has been through enough lately.

"Yeah…" she says quietly, her voice clearer than before. "Danny did mention about a couple of guys he'd noticed around the college. He thought they might have been following him."

"Did he tell you what they looked like?" I ask, trying to keep the adrenal rush of recognition from intruding on my voice.

"I think…" she starts, slowly, trying to recall. "Yeah… a couple of dogs in sharp suits. Dobermans, I think he said. He'd said they'd been hanging around the gym and the quad, like they were waiting for somebody. He saw them a few times over a couple of days; that's what made him think that…"

Mary's voice trails off as the sudden realization of what might have happened to her erstwhile boyfriend hits her like a freight train. More tears well up in her eyes. I'm surprised she has any left. She abruptly turns her head away, towards the stage once more, and I can hear her sobbing. Even Ramona has been shocked into sobriety, no longer leaning drunkenly on my arm, cupping the wineglass in her dainty hands and just staring into the liquid. The band is still playing, slow and quiet in the stillness.

"I don't think I want this anymore," Ramona finally says, breaking the silence, and in a much better state than I was expecting. "I need to powder my nose. I'll see you outside, Mr. Llewellyn."

The raccoon stands from her perch, stumbling less than I'd imagined she would, and makes her way to the ladies' room, leaving Mary and me alone at the table. The young cat slowly turns her topaz-yellow eyes to me, her face scrunched up in anguish and sorrow.

"Did they…?" she begins to say, the words catching in her throat. I get what she's trying to ask me — "Did they kill Danny?" A little knot of guilt forms in the pit of my stomach.

"I can't really tell you," I say in response. I really can't tell her. I don't want to jeopardize the whole investigation by having an emotionally distraught girl with a deep connection to one of my leads getting in the way. Even though there's nothing tangible directly linking Danny to the missing Ayani Onyelé, I have a gut feeling that the two incidents are connected. Unfortunately, that hunch is currently sharing a living space with that guilty knot I've got. Before I can say any more, Mary has leapt up from her seat, knocking the chair onto its back, anger and sadness clashing in her eyes, the pupils forming tiny, hateful slits.

"You have to tell me!" she screeches, every syllable echoing. An absolute silence falls over the club as those five words continue to thrum in my ears. The band has suddenly stopped playing. The few remaining eyes around us are all staring in our direction, illuminated like lanterns. I can already hear the heavy tramp of the bouncer making his way over. Mary notices everyone staring.

"What are you lookin' at?" she shouts at the assembled crowd, and they all slink back, embarrassed. Pleasant kid. Before either of us can make another move, I feel a weighty hand on my shoulder. I turn my head, looking up into the brawny face of the moose bouncer, in his stark white shirt and slick bowtie that can barely contain his thick neck, his huge antlers blocking out the already subdued lights above us.

"Trouble, sir, eh?" he asks in a bass rumble,

"No, no trouble at all, pal," I say, trying to defuse the situation. "She's just a bit, er… emotional…"

"I can see that, sir," the moose replies, as deadpan as you please. "Everyone can."

I nod sheepishly and let out a little chuckle. Mary is still fuming with rage. I gently remove the bouncer's hand from my shoulder and stand up, overbalancing, but manage to catch myself.

"We were just leaving," I say to him. "It's been a long night."

"Good idea, sir," the moose replies, still expressionless, his tone flatter than a deadbeat dad. I motion for Mary to come with me. Though she's still mad, she picks up her bag and coat, the jagged edge of anger covering every movement, and reluctantly follows, obviously knowing when she's been beaten. The low murmur of talk resumes as we leave the Unity Club, and I make a mental note to avoid the place for a while. It's a shame. The band tonight was good, from what little I heard. Seems like a nice place to hang out if I'm ever on this side of the river again. We walk through the entrance hall, an uncomfortable quiet following our steps, and make our way outside. At least out here, she can't embarrass herself publicly, not with how quiet the streets have become. There's not another soul around. Her eyes flash at me as I'm lighting my cigarette.

"You have to tell me..." she says to me again in a low, threatening hiss. She'd have to try harder than that on most days, but I relent, knowing that it'd get her off my back. Besides, I don't want to be on the receiving end of a cat's claws.

"All the evidence is leading in that direction," I say to her. "Packsters may have killed your beau. But I really can't say if those particular dogs were involved. The ones that had been around your boyfriend on the night in question are already filling lockers at the morgue. Can't be sure about the guys that might have been following Danny."

"Good..." she whispers, almost inaudible, but picked up

by my dog hearing. I suddenly feel the atmosphere grow colder, like she's about to pounce and claw my throat out. One dog is as good as the next, she's probably thinking. She's spent two days crying over a boy; her mental state isn't going to be exactly stable. At this point, Ramona comes through the huge swinging doors to meet us.

"Man," Ramona says, almost too jovially. "Didn't think you'd be out front already! You could have told me!"

The atmosphere changes once again, the chill tangibly sapping from the air like it had never even existed. The smoke exits my lips, and I don't even register that I'd been holding my breath. I proffer the cigarette to Mary, but she refuses.

"I've got my own," she says, exhausted, pulling a cigarette from somewhere in her purse, the gold band around the filter gleaming in the guttering glow of the streetlights. I say nothing as she lights up. A few moments and a few puffs of smoke pass before Mary speaks again.

"Thank you," she says quietly.

"No problem," I reply. "But why are you thanking me?"

"Like you said, tonight's helped me clear my head," she says, her eyes no longer so sorrowful. "I think I can go past this… well, as long as no more reporters come looking for me."

"I've got a friend works for the Herald," I say, despite knowing that I can't be sure of that. "I'll pass along the message to leave you alone."

Mary takes a long drag on the high-class cigarette she's sporting, the smoke leaving her in a slow, shivering breath. She's still not over this, I think, but at least it's a good start, and I won't have to worry about her causing trouble. Ramona, for the third time tonight, breaks the tension.

"Listen," she says, putting a hand on Mary's arm. "If you need someone to talk to… or anything… y'know?"

Mary nods in agreement, a tiny smile finally playing its way across her face.

"I'll be fine," she says. "But thank you. I'll think about it."

It always amazes me how, even in the deepest and most dire of tragedies, it's always possible to find a new friend. I think I just witnessed that right now between these two girls who are probably no older than I was when I joined the Police Academy. It's kind of touching, really. Still, we can't all stand around exchanging feelings until sun-up. We say our goodbyes to Mary, with Ramona giving her one last hug, and she heads out into the Oldsburg night, back to her sorority house. We head in the opposite direction. I'll walk Ramona back home, then find a payphone to call Sid. I've got a lot to write down in my notebook once I get back to my apartment.

It's near enough four in the morning as I'm virtually dragging Ramona back to her dorm. The booze seems to have reasserted itself in her system because she's gurgling and slurring like I can't tell you. She's leaning heavily on my arm, almost too heavy given her frame, but I'm a strong guy. At least it's the left arm and not the right. If that were the case, I'd be in real trouble. The going is slow, too, given her choice of footwear and how badly she's weaving. Stilettos and heavy drinking really don't mix. I'm actually surprised she hasn't taken her shoes off by now. This strangely reminds me of how Jenny and I used to be when we were younger, especially after a tough week. A lot of booze, a few carefree laughs, maybe a long kiss under a streetlight somewhere. I sigh to myself as the memories flash through my mind. I miss those times, but I know I'll never get those days back. Check me getting all sentimental, huh?

There are only a couple of lights on in Ramona's building by the time we get there, and one of those is in the lobby. The two oxen who were standing guard all night have been replaced by an aged ferret who seems to be having trouble staying awake, sat comfortably at the reception desk. He's probably there more to keep a watch on the place than to stop any rowdy behavior, and it shows. We stop at the door, and Ramona detaches herself from my arm before getting a familiar look on her face, one I've seen far too many times. She's trying to come on to me. I can sense the distinct aroma of drunken libido, not to mention smell it on her breath as she draws in close to me.

"Wanna come up w'th me, m'ster private d'tective?" she slurs at me. I raise an eyebrow at the question and throw a little nod towards the security guard.

"I don't think your house-mother would be too impressed," I say to her, trying to let her down gently. She just brushes that comment off like it was nothing.

"He won' mind," she says, sly as her species is known to be, desperately trying to be seductive. "Come on up an' have a li'l fun w'th me…"

If I were anything like some of the older guys we'd seen tonight, I'd have jumped at the chance. Still, I'm no slimy creep, so I answer the only way I can.

"You're too young for me, kid," I say flatly. She doesn't take this too well. If anything, she takes it as an insult.

"Didn't have a problem when these charlies wuz up in y'r face th' oth'r night," she says defensively, grabbing her boobs and thrusting them at me. I don't rise to the bait. She knows I've seen them already, anyway.

"That was strictly business," I say, matter-of-factly. "This right here isn't. You're a sweet kid, and you've got a good head on your shoulders, but I'm gonna have to decline."

"Well... y'r loss, buster..." she sighs, pouting and turning to the door, going only a few faltering steps before she pauses in her tracks. She turns back unsteadily, and looks fixedly at me.

"Ya gots somethin' on y'r face, y'know?" She says, approaching me again. I barely have time to register the comment before she hugs me and plants a big kiss on my cheek, barely skipping a beat in what, for her, is probably one of the funniest practical jokes she's pulled on anyone, ever.

"My lips!" she shouts, a big smile across her face, the small amount of lipstick she's still wearing already smeared against my furry mug. I can't help but laugh along with her as she wishes me good night and heads inside. I stand there, still chuckling, and look at my watch. It's coming up to four thirty in the morning, and I need to get home. I'd better find a payphone and see if Sid's still on shift to come and pick me up. It'll probably be difficult to explain the lipstick to him, though.

It doesn't take long for Sid to drop me back home, and, yeah, he asked me where I'd got the smacker from. I simply told him that a gentleman doesn't kiss and tell, to which he remarked, "Since when were you ever a gentleman?" We had a quiet laugh about it, but I held my tongue.

I ask him if he's had a busy night, and he says I'm his last customer, after which we sit in silence while the cold light of pre-dawn starts to creep over the skyscrapers. Even the majority of the traffic has disappeared for the night, though in this city, there are still a few cars on the road, some animal needing to be somewhere even at this benighted hour of the morning, and soon enough, we pull up outside my apartment building. It's almost eerily quiet. I guess even Eduardo has to sleep sometime. I pay for the lift, and Sid pulls away, headed for his own home. I climb those familiar steel stairs, my limbs heavy with fatigue, every step laborious. I reach into my pocket for my keys and unlock my door. It's good to be home after such a wild night, but I can't go to sleep just yet. I need to get my thoughts down in my notebook before I can do that.

I open the door and turn on the lights, shutting the door behind me before shuffling over to my desk, where my notebook rests, the tattered pages still open to where I left the most recent case notes. Might need to get a new notebook; this one's looking thin. I pick up a pen with my left hand, trying desperately not to smudge the ink as I scrawl down what I've learned over the course of the evening.

From what I've learned from Mary Lansing, her former boyfriend Daniel Arden had suspicions of being followed, specifically by Dobermans in suits. Those jokers could have been Ziggy, Rocco, that Paulie guy, or any other members of the Donati pack, but I can't be certain. Maybe that's what started the fight at the Watering Hole: Danny could have recognized them and confronted them about it, at which point things got ugly. Alternatively, he was probably so paranoid about being followed that it was a case of mistaken identity. Everything about what was going through his head is still pretty conjectural. I write down my thoughts, just before the tiredness and alcohol kick in.

I wake up, still dressed in what I was wearing the night before, flat on my back and staring at the ceiling. Bright, glaring sunshine beams through the windows of my apartment, too bright for my hungover eyes. How did this happen? As I move my heavy limbs, I realize I'm in my bed that I must have folded out of the wall. I have a hazy recollection of cleaning up enough to bring it down. Must have been running on autopilot, I guess. It's not too far-fetched of an idea. What surprises me more is that the nightmares hadn't come. I raise my watch to my bleary eyes, not even having the strength to lift my head to look at my wall clock. Nearly nine in the morning. Oh well, some rest is better than none. I consider setting myself down for a few more hours until I realize I've got far too much that I need to do. I get up slowly, so that the top of my head doesn't fall off, sitting on the edge of the fold-out bed, taking a few deep breaths. My mouth feels like it's growing its own beard, and my eyes feel like two clumps of sage-brush. I know I drink every day, but this is an unwelcome surprise even for me. What day is it again? I've lost track of time, not an uncommon tendency in those who drink.

Saturday, that's it. It's Saturday. I rub my eyes with my good hand, trying to get them working properly, blinking hard every now and then. I start to stand but think better of it as my knees crack dramatically beneath my weight. I slump back into a sitting position and try again, finally managing to get myself upright. I shuffle slowly to the bathroom, which seems like it's a million miles away, and turn on the sink faucets. A few splashes of water across my face, and I feel a bit more alive. I also make a point of scrubbing Ramona's lipstick out of my cheek, though it takes a little time. I'm thirsty, too, but I know

137

better than to drink the water in this building, and the bottle of bourbon on my desk is empty. I sigh, my breath feeling like a blast furnace and smelling like a brewery. Guess I'll need to head out and buy more. At least some fresh air should help.

I can't be bothered to change just yet, so I just grab my trench coat and hat, making my way outside to the street. It's surprisingly sunny today, though there's still that early-Spring nip in the air, the one that constantly sticks around until you're almost into Summer. It's also busy, the traffic forming a constant stream as the Saturday rush-hour grinds on, exhaust fumes and car horns mingling around me in a bid to see which one can discomfit me more given the state I'm in. I try to block it out through sheer force of willpower, until I finally get to the convenience store on the corner, an oasis in a desert of hungover nausea. I don't even bother picking up a paper, simply asking for a forty of bourbon and a pack of smokes, before plucking a bottle of mineral water from one of the refrigerators and buying that too.

"Heavy night, thir?" the duck at the counter lisps at me. I'm still sure he's related to the one I see normally.

"You could say that," I reply. "I'd rather not talk about it."

"Thorry, thir," he says, the syllables still sloppy and lisping. "Not really my buthineth anyway. Have a nithe day, now!"

I thank him and head back to my apartment, idly sipping at the water to clear my mouth as I walk. The liquid is refreshing and cool, simple purity, something I could really use right now, especially after the sleazy underbelly of the student scene last night. It was definitely something I could have done without, at least physically, but now a few pieces are falling into place.

I head back indoors, where the harsh light of the sun can be blocked out with a blind, and sit myself at my desk. I look at the bottle of bourbon in my hand, casually discarding the brown paper bag I was carrying it in. Just another bit of trash to clean up sometime never, I guess. I could seriously use a quick slug just to not totally feel like crap. Hair of the dog that bit you, if you'll pardon the expression. However, I decide against it. If I'm going to be talking to anybody at the Zebra Nation embassy, I'll need to keep a clear head, or at least as clear as it's going to get today. I call up city information and ask if the embassy has a public phone number. Fortunately for me, it does, so I scribble it down, as best I can left-handed, and hang up before lifting the receiver again and dialing. It's a few minutes until a female voice comes over the phone. By the accent, I'm guessing she's Zebra Nation herself, possibly a secretary.

"Good morning. Zebra Nation Embassy," she states. "How may I help you?"

"Yeah, I need to see one of the visiting diplomats," I say to her. "It's kind of important."

"Name, please?" she asks. I hadn't expected that, so I go along with it.

"Rex Llewellyn," I say. "I'm… working on something for Ms Onyelé. There's been a development."

I hear a rustle of papers across the line. Sounds like this secretary is looking for something. A few tense moments go by before she answers again.

"Ah… yes," she says. "We were informed that you might be calling soon, Mr. Llewellyn. Mistress Onyelé is busy this afternoon, but I can schedule for her to see you this evening, out of working hours. She seemed most eager to see you privately."

"That'd be grand, thanks," I sigh, relieved. Seems getting an appointment at the embassy was easier than I thought, and since it's out of hours, I won't have to worry about anyone uninvited dropping in. The secretary tells me what time; seven thirty p.m. I thank her and hang up, searching in my pocket for my smokes and lighting up. That gives me a few hours to kill. There's nothing else really weighing on my mind right now, so I guess I should try to unwind from the investigation for a while. Though the cigarette doesn't help my hungover state much, I consider my options for what to do in my downtime.

Sam's place? No, that's a bad idea at this time of day, especially if I'll be there tomorrow anyway, Tilton or not. Read yesterday's paper again? I don't really feel like it, and I probably wouldn't be able to concentrate on it anyway. Maybe I should head down to the Bijou and take in a movie or two? As much as I hate to admit it, that sounds like the best option. I change into one of my usual suits and head out.

The Bijou movie theatre is a majestic old building on the northern side of the Bowery, worn by time and weather, but not diminished in its grandeur. It used to be a vaudeville house back in its time, before the day of the motion picture came around, and the performing arts fizzled out into virtual nonexistence. My grandpa used to bring Jerome and me here when we were pups, to see whatever stage act was performing that night, usually the sillier, slapstick comedians, and humorous narrations that always flew over our young heads, but always got a chuckle out of Grandpa Owain. When he died, Mom would bring us, but it just wasn't the same. A lot of the old fixtures and fittings still remain, with the lobby sporting an arched ceiling and gilt trims, and frescoes adorning a small rotunda. The only real difference now is the marquee out front that proclaims whatever new Tinseltown epic is currently showing, the garishly colorful movie posters that adorn the entranceway, each showing off a different star, and the colossal silver screen in the main auditorium.

Although the brisk walk has cleared the hangover well enough, I realize, too late, that it's Saturday afternoon. That means the kids' matinee is on. I inwardly cringe at the thought, but I really have nothing better to do, so I pay my money and head into the darkened theatre. Everywhere there are children of all species, kicking up a ruckus fit to wake the dead, and among them, the embarrassed faces of far too many long-suffering Fathers and Mothers, just praying that the afternoon passes quickly. The playbill is mainly comprised of short cartoons, mostly from the Preston Brothers studio, alongside a couple of B-grade Westerns, some science fiction serial that I could honestly not care less about, and one newsreel. Not a terrible billing, to be fair, for the kids on a weekend.

I decide to make the best of it and find a seat near the aisle at the back. It'd pay well to have those ankle-biters in front of me, just so I don't get a spit-ball to the back of the head. I reach into my pocket for a cigarette but decide against it. Don't want some angry parent giving me grief for smoking in front of their child. They're changing reels between cartoons, so the noise of those little monsters is unbearable, but soon enough, the next cartoon is on, and the familiar PB logo comes careening up onto the enormous screen, alongside the studio's catchy jingle. A sudden hush falls, every one of the kids enraptured by whatever shenanigans Murray Moose and his buddies are getting up to this week, occasionally breaking out into riotous laughter. The jokes are good, and I even find myself laughing occasionally. But I pick up something else among the laughter, a familiar voice, deep and resonant.

I pause and look around, only to see Bill, the ox that I met the other day, further along the row of seats, roaring with laughter even harder than any of the brats assembled in the auditorium. I really hope that he doesn't spot me. I don't think I could handle a conversation with him right now. I don't have the mental capacity for it. I also wonder to myself what he's doing at a Saturday matinee by himself, but I guess it's probably the cartoons, a case of simple pleasures for simple minds. He's sitting in as rapt fascination of the screen as the kids are, so I'm probably right. It seems we're the only two adults in the place unaccompanied by a child; me for a bad call of judgment, and him because he seems to want to be here. I once again try to make the best of it, sitting as quietly as I can in my seat, at least trying to get to the newsreel. That at least could be informative.

After a couple more cartoons and at least one shower of thrown popcorn from some little twerp, the newsreel starts. A lot about the Tinseltown jet set, a news story about whatever military coup is happening in St. Roch-knows-where, some sports news (baseball and motor-racing, no less), but nothing really eye-catching. That is until they get to the news from the Capitol. My ears prick up, and I sit forward, trying to hear past the frustrated mewling of the kids around me. There's President Milstrom all right, the fat pigeon himself, shaking hands with a male zebra in a fancy caftan and serious-looking, round-framed glasses. My eyes widen as I hear the name Onyelé and see the family resemblance. He has the same stripe pattern as both Ziva and Ayani, if I'm not imagining it. I really wish I could hear the rest of the report, but even my acute hearing can't penetrate the barrier of caterwauling children around me.

I decide to step out for a smoke before the reel finishes. I'd been itching for one for a while. Besides, that crazy sci-fi nonsense was coming up next, and it's not really my thing. I light the cigarette and take a few drags, the nicotine burning through my veins and softening the world. Man, I needed that. The rumble of the Saturday afternoon traffic around me seems to have a calming effect, too, at least in dispelling the sound of those squealing brats in the theatre. I barely hear the heavy clomp of feet behind me, and I turn to see Bill looming over me like he did the other night. I jump at the sight of him but regain my composure. I guess a tall, imposing animal like him must have this effect on a lot of others. He smiles a big, slow smile as the light of recognition dawns on him.

"Hey, Mr. Loolin," he rumbles to me in a friendly manner. "You come to the picture show too?"

Guess the big lug still hasn't learned to pronounce my name yet.

"Oh, hey Bill," I say to him. "Yeah… just thought I'd see what was on."

"Funny cartoons. Always my favorite," he says simply.

Great. Now I'm stuck with this guy. I don't dislike him, but it takes an awful lot of patience to be around him, something I have in very short supply at the moment. I'd make a gracious exit, but I don't know how this big dumb ox will take it.

"You doin' anything this afternoon, Mr. Loolin?" he asks. The question comes entirely out of nowhere and kind of knocks me for a loop. Why would he ask that? I answer cautiously.

"Not really… why?"

"Wanted to talk some more with you," he says. "Mama found some of Hank's things. Thought they might help."

"Really…?" I say carefully. This could help, but I'm not too sure if that's the case. Still, Bill seems genuine enough - I don't think he really has the brains to be devious – and I've got nothing better to do for a few more hours anyway. I definitely can't face going back inside with all those snot-nosed kids causing a riot. I can trust this guy. He hasn't steered me wrong in the past.

"Okay, pal," I say to him. "Lead on."

At this, Bill turns with all the speed of a grindstone and lumbers off down the street in huge, plodding strides. I take to my heels so as not to lose him in the busy, crowded streets of the Bowery.

It's not an awfully long walk before we come to the house that belongs to Bill's mother. It's a simple, shingle building out in the suburbs of the Pastures that's obviously seen better days, the paint cracking and peeling from the walls in long strips, the front yard overgrown with weeds, so much so that I wonder if I'll need a machete to get to the front door. A moth-eaten couch, the cushions long gone and the springs sticking up through the upholstery, sits forlornly on the sidewalk by the rusted, chain-link gate leading to the path. I guess garbage day around here isn't for a while yet, if it ever comes.

Bill moves ahead of me like a walking continent, opening the gate with one of those massive hands, the unoiled hinges squealing in protest, and I follow close behind. He leads me along the cracked concrete path to the front porch, a screen door standing silently in front of us. Behind the usual distant hum of traffic and street noise, I can hear the faint sound of a radio coming from within. Sounds like a soap opera in progress, if I'm not mistaken. Quietly, Bill produces a key from his pocket that looks almost comically tiny in his huge fist. He moves aside the screen and unlocks the door. The noise of the radio suddenly gets a lot louder, and the musty scent of the elderly wafts along on the light, mid-afternoon breeze.

The interior of the house is somewhat better kept than the exterior, but it still has a worn-out feeling, a family home that had probably been so for generations of cows and oxen. Faded, framed photographs line every wall, the sepia, bovine characters in each staring blankly out from across the years, each one as sturdy as a redwood. Bill's family, I guess. The rest of the décor is drab but in good order, and my initial suspicions were correct about it being a soap opera on the radio. The old girl probably likes listening to her stories.

"Ma!" Bill yells like a boom of thunder. "We got company!"

I hear the radio quiet down, and a low shuffling coming from the parlor, punctuated by a couple of quiet thuds on the threadbare carpet every few seconds. Then she rounds the corner, Bill's mother, an aged heifer with sagging skin and fine, tightly curled white hair, supported by two walking sticks. The calves of her legs seem to have merged with her ankles, and every bit of them that shows below her dress is riddled with varicose veins, contrasting horribly with the tartan slippers she's wearing. A hearing aid is wedged firmly in her left ear, an old cattle tag dangling from the right one. Her back is curved more like a bow than a spine, which explains the sticks. Still, despite the filmy sheen on her eyes, she recognizes and greets her son with a bright smile, and the big guy bends down to embrace her, more gently than I thought he could ever manage. She finally notices me standing awkwardly next to Bill, and a hint of suspicion crosses her wrinkled face.

"Who's this fella, son?" she croaks to Bill, her voice worn with age.

"This that Mr. Loolin, ma," says Bill. "The one I told you 'bout. He come to see Hank's things."

"It's Llewellyn, actually, ma'am," I say to her. "I'm a private detective."

Though she still has that suspicious look, she nods slowly and turns back towards the parlor.

"The shamus, eh?" she says as she shuffles her way unsteadily to the parlor door, before calling over her shoulder, "And less of the ma'am. Just call me Betsy. Everyone else does. And don't just be standing there waiting for the grass to grow; come have a seat!"

Bill and I follow her into the front room, and despite all of the furniture being as worn and aged as the house's occupant, everything is neatly arranged and well cared for, even down to the hand-crocheted doilies that cover every arm of every chair. A tall cabinet with a glass front faces the door, assorted knick-knacks and porcelain figurines filling the shelves, but on the top shelf stand several urns, incongruous among the otherwise light-hearted novelties. Despite the fine layer of dust along most of the surfaces in here, the urns are spotless. I cast a cursory look towards the containers, each elaborately carved or painted, no two the same, reading names like Arthur, Leslie, and Ida, along with their birth and death dates. Standing at the forefront, though, is one upon which the name Hank has been etched, brand new. Why do I suddenly feel a pang of guilt for even looking?

Betsy crosses to a raised chair by the radio, where she probably spends most of her time, and sits down heavily, every bone and muscle in her elderly frame creaking worse than mine, before propping her walking sticks by the wall next to her. I wait for Bill to sit, but he doesn't, so I sit in an armchair close to his mother, so I can be heard, if the hearing aid is any indicator. Bill plods over to a different chair, his footfalls heavy on the carpet, the urns atop the cabinet rattling gently with each tread, their occupants clearly in no state to complain. I turn to Betsy and sigh. Seems she's known a great deal of loss in her lifetime.

"I'm sorry for your loss, ma- uh… Betsy…" I say, still not used to saying the name. In the detective game, it's always a good idea to keep a professional distance and to — usually — be on first-name terms only with clients, so this is strange to me.

"What?" she says, overly loudly. Damn, must have been speaking too quietly. I repeat what I said, a little louder than before, but without raising my voice to a shout. Betsy grumbles an acknowledgment before speaking again.

"Yes… Hank… terrible that he had that accident. We're still waiting for the crematory to give us a call, so we can pick him up," she says, sadly, but I know this isn't her first rodeo, so to speak. There are no tears, not even a waver in her voice. Even though Hank was her son, it makes me wonder just how long it takes, with so much death around you, before it loses its sting.

"You have a few of his things that I might need to take a look at," I say, turning on the soulful eyes. "It might help with what I'm currently investigating."

"I know," she says. "I'm not deaf, you know."

She motions to Bill, and he stands from his chair, making his way out the door and, guessing by the heavy footsteps, up the stairs. Betsy turns to me, a kindlier look on her face than before.

"You really must stay with us for lunch, Mr. Llewellyn," she says. "You look like you haven't eaten in a week. I've got a nut-roast in the oven. Plenty of potatoes and carrots, too."

The thing that surprises me more than the offer of a square meal is that she's pronounced my name correctly, but from my experience, cows tend to have a bit more between their ears than their menfolk do. At the mention of the roast, though, my nose pricks up, and there is indeed a heavenly smell of cooking coming from somewhere within the house. It's herbivore food, sure, but my mouth starts to water anyway.

"I'd be glad to, Betsy," I say graciously. "Thank you."

At this, I hear Bill's plodding tread descending the stairs, and he rounds the corner into the room holding a beaten-up old shoebox that probably once held something the Statue of Harmony could squeeze into. These must be Hank's former possessions. Before I can say anything, though, Betsy pipes up to her son.

"Set another place at the table, would you, son? Mr. Llewellyn is going to be joining us."

Bill simply smiles a slow smile.

It's several hours later when we finally finish eating, even though my messed-up paw made things a little difficult. Though the roast was overdone and crumbling to pieces, I didn't particularly care. It was probably the first decent meal I'd had in a while that didn't come in a take-out box. As I'd suspected, it was herbivore food; several types of freshly boiled vegetables, baked potatoes slathered in butter, corn on the cob, and the flaking nut-roast taking pride of place despite being cooked for too long.

The only reason the meal took as long as it did is that Betsy has a tendency to chew slowly and methodically, a usual bovine trait (and unsurprising given her advanced age and lack of teeth), alongside her motherly tendency to dish out several helpings to both me and Bill. In Bill's case, I can see why, and what made him such a big boy in the first place. As for myself, I can already feel the waistband of my pants uncomfortably stretching to its limits. I loosen my belt by a few notches and graciously decline a fourth helping while Bill helps his mother clear away the dishes and flatware. Then, though hazed by being overly full, my mind wanders back to the contents of the coffin-sized shoebox in the front parlor. I'm still doubtful that Bill's late brother, Hank, had anything of use to my investigation, but I guess I'm about to find out.

Bill, Betsy, and I all head back into the parlor, and I slump contentedly into a chair before once again broaching the subject of the box's contents. Bill silently hands it to me, and I lift the cardboard lid that some West Coast surfer could have tackled some serious waves on. Inside the box are several envelopes and pieces of paper, a few photos, and odd bits and pieces of other detritus. I notice a faded vacation photo of Bill, Betsy, and another ox that I can only assume to be Hank, standing in front of what looks like Echo Valley, out in the Midwestern territories. The two brothers loom like giants wearing gaudy Los Vargas t-shirts, their mother looking ridiculously shrunken and small between them in her horn-rimmed glasses and sun visor, clutching the cracked rubber handles of a walking frame.

I quietly put the photo back in the box and continue rifling through the contents. Betsy is already snoring in her chair as I search. My fingers brush over an envelope that doesn't seem like the others, much daintier than one that would be delivered to a bovine. My brow knitting, I pull the envelope from its place and see a typed name on the front:

Ayani Onyelé.

My heart leaps at the discovery. How did Hank come into possession of this? More curious than wise, I check to see if anything is inside, and sure enough, a small, thick note has been hastily stuffed there, partially creased and screwed up. I ask Bill about it, and he replies that he doesn't know anything about it.

"Hank prob'ly meant to give it to someone," Bill says slowly. "Must be for them. Don't know who, though."

I know exactly who it's meant for, but I don't think it was Hank who wrote it. I pocket the note and keep looking, resolving to read it later. My hands find an address book among the contents of the box. I open the pages and see that there are a lot of names, addresses, and phone numbers in there, mostly from females. I scan my eyes over the walls of text and notice Amber's name among them, and Ramona's, but I don't see Ayani anywhere. I breathe a disappointed sigh. A dead-end again, but a thought comes to my mind. This, in my hands, is a valuable source of information on everyone who works at the Watering Hole. It seems Hank was looking out for the employees' safety even if Jock just saw them as a way to make money, and I give a tiny smile at that noble sentiment. This could come in handy, even if I have to go through every number and charge my phone bill up the ass to find something.

"Can I keep this?" I ask Bill, holding up the book,

"Anything you need, Mr. Loolin," says Bill.

I tuck the book into an inside pocket, though it's pretty thick and strains the seams slightly. Another quick rummage turns up nothing more of real interest, and I put the enormous lid back on the equally enormous box. I place it quietly on the floor beside me and stand up, my knees creaking under the strain of all the extra weight of food I'm carrying. The light outside is gradually turning a golden orange, shot through with pink clouds. I need to get home, gather my evidence, and smarten myself up before meeting Ziva at the embassy. I cross the parlor, Betsy still sleeping peacefully where she sits, and Bill follows me to the door, but not before scribbling something on a piece of paper. I hear the lead of the pencil scratching and crackling before Bill hands it to me. It's a phone number. I look puzzled at the big ox, but he already seems to know what I'm going to ask.

"It our number here," he says dully. "I'mma stay with ma a few days. You need me, just call."

I thank him, and he gently closes the door behind him. I decide to muddle my way back through the streets of the Pastures to the Bijou and head home from there. As I walk along the broken concrete sidewalks, I reach into my pocket for the little note that I pulled out of the shoebox; the one addressed very plainly to Ayani. I stop and look around myself to make sure I'm not being watched before opening the envelope and reading the message. As I do, a chill runs through me, that even the setting sun can't warm. The words are a hodgepodge of letters cut from various newspapers and magazines, a typical tactic for threatening notes, and virtually untraceable. It reads:

"We know where you are staying. Do not try to run. It would be a shame if an accident were to befall you. What would your father say? We will be in touch."

I give it a quick sniff, and apart from the strong smell of the paste used to affix the letters, there are four other smells: the cheap dog pheromones I know from previously; the scent of an actual dog, possibly a Doberman; sea-salt; and the faint tang of the gasoline they used to destroy any fingerprints from the original sender. I stuff the note back into its envelope, thrust it back into my pocket, and walk away, more quickly than I'd intended. I've got that uneasy feeling in my dander that something rotten is afoot.

After getting home and changing into something more formal, I head out to the Zebra Nation embassy. It's on the West side of the Holbrook, in Oakwood Heights, where many of the political institutions of Oldsburg reside, including City Hall. It's a high-class neighborhood, where the guy having his back scratched is usually keeping a close eye on the one doing the scratching. The police patrols in this district are doubled as a matter of course, with so many diplomats and political figures in one space. I get an uneasy feeling being around so many cops that I could have worked with, but the feeling passes quickly.

Tucked under my arm, in a brown paper bag liberated from a booze bottle, is all the physical evidence I've collected so far: the bloody clothes, the purse with its Spirit Key, the note. I'm hoping Ziva will take my word for what I've seen and heard, but I'm also thinking she has a softer, more innocent view of her little sister. The photo she showed me originally backs that theory up.

It's late into the evening, the glowing orange of sunset replaced by a sapphire blue as the moon starts to rise, but I'm still ahead of schedule. Never leave a lady waiting, especially one with powerful political connections. It's a good thing that Sid dropped me off nearby with what little I could pay him, but there's still a fair walk to the Embassy, at least from what I could find out.

I turn the corner of Persian and 12th, and there it is; an imposing edifice of brick and marble, surrounded by a high wall. The flag of the Zebra Nation is flying listlessly from a flagpole beside the flag of the Federated States of Newland. Compared to the simple red, white, and blue of our own banner, the red, green, black, and white in diagonal, clashing stripes is particularly jarring, not to mention the image of a ceremonial mask firmly in the center. As I look up at the flags, a creeping feeling of familiarity comes over me, but of what eludes me. I shiver slightly from the rapidly cooling night air and approach the high, wrought-iron gates leading to the main driveway. Beyond them, I can see a beautifully kept garden of gravel pathways and exotic flowers and grasses such as don't grow natively to Oldsburg, or anywhere else in this country. If, as I suspect, they were taken wholesale from the Zebra Nation, they must be pretty hardy to survive the change of climate, so different from the veldts and savannahs that they're native to.

There's an intercom buzzer by the gate, and I press the button. There's no sound, but a small, green light flashes for a moment, so I know something must have happened. A few seconds later, a female voice comes scratchily over the system. It's the receptionist I spoke to over the phone, in her usual business-like manner.

"Name and business, please?" she says.

"It's Rex Llewellyn," I say. "I'm here for my seven thirty with Ms Onyelé."

A brief rustling of papers from the intercom tells me she's looking up my appointment. I wait patiently.

"All right, Mr. Llewellyn. I'll send someone to lead you in." She says finally before cutting off communication. I don't know how long I'll have to wait, so I fish a cigarette out of my pocket and put it between my lips. I needn't have bothered. Just as I'm reaching for my lighter, the guard arrives. It's not that he's a zebra that takes me aback, but his costume.

He wears a brightly patterned toga of gold, emerald-green, and blood-red that makes a counterpoint to the black and white stripes of his skin. Copious amounts of bangles of various precious metals wrap his lithe, wiry arms, and he carries a long spear, several feathers and clumps of hair fluttering from the haft in the cool night breeze. Around his neck is a leather thong attached to a knag of wood, his Spirit Key. He also wears a serious expression on his face as he wordlessly opens the gate and gestures for me to follow him. I guess that, since the embassy is sovereign soil, and with the ambassador and his family in residence, an honor guard in full regalia isn't out of the question, and this guy's one of them. I quietly walk behind him, my shoes crunching on the gravel as we go, the only sound around us, a sense of foreboding following me. Why isn't my escort making a sound?

We reach the plate-glass doors of the embassy, and I notice four more zebras dressed and armed in similar fashion, two males, two females, just as stone-silent as my guide. I follow as he strides through the doors, which part before him, right up to the reception desk, before he taps the butt of his spear twice on the pale marble floor and takes his leave. The echo reverberates uncannily around the vast, open hall, decorated in native artwork and woodcarvings. I barely have time to admire it all before the receptionist speaks to me.

"Mr. Llewellyn?" She inquires.

"Uh… yeah…" I reply absently, almost lost in the grandiose scale of the entrance hall. "That's me…"

"Mr. Pettibone will be with you shortly," she says. "And he will take you to Mistress Onyelé. She has been most eager to see you, in fact."

"Yeah… you said," I reply. Though my fur bristles slightly at the mention of Pettibone, I can't help but feel a sense of satisfaction at the investigation so far. I've got something solid to present to Ziva, which I'm hoping is more than Jen has. The receptionist smiles at me, a big, professional smile full of pearly white teeth. The last time I saw a smile that big, a crocodile was on the other end of it.

"Would you like to take a seat, Mr. Llewellyn?" She asks, and I nod dumbly, taking a chair by the desk. I feel thoroughly out of place here. I'm just a gumshoe with too many years on the street and too many dog biscuits under his belt. My usual racket is uncovering the truth behind thefts, murders, missing relatives, and cheating spouses amongst the animals of Oldsburg, but this is the arena of high international politics. A place like this embassy has the tendency to make a guy feel incredibly small, almost insignificant. I mean, I've had a couple of moderately well-off clients in the past, but this is a whole other ballgame. I shuffle nervously in my seat.

Before too many minutes have passed, the quiet is broken by the measured, steady pace of overly shiny shoes across the marble, shoes that contain a small body. I look up to see Pettibone gliding through the hall, dressed in a severe grey suit, his tiny eyeglasses flashing as he passes each wall-lamp. Before long, he's reached me, clicking his heels together formally, looking up at me.

"It is good to see you, Mr. Llewellyn," he says, with the trained formality you would expect. "If you would follow me, please."

He turns on his heel, barely allowing me to raise my bulk out of the chair, cracking knees and all, before leading me further into the Embassy's foyer. At the back of the huge room, we stand and wait for an elevator in silence, me shuffling uneasily, the bag under my arm feeling like it weighs a ton, what with all the damage it might cause. This guy still puts my teeth on edge, and not necessarily because of his cold disposition. There's just something I can't put my finger on. The doors open, and we both get into the elevator, the polished brass fittings doing nothing to put me at ease. He pushes the button for our floor, and the familiar lurch of going up hits my stomach. There's a good long silence, but it's Pettibone who speaks first as we ride up.

"I must say, it's good to see you in a more sober mood, Mr. Llewellyn," he says, a tiny smile on his tiny face. It immediately gets on my nerves.

"And what's that supposed to mean, short-stuff?" I ask, my tone somewhere between defensive and irritated. For the briefest second, his cool demeanor flusters.

"My apologies, sir, I meant no offense," he starts. "I was just saying, sir."

"Yeah, well, there's plenty offense taken, buddy," I reply. "I get enough crap from you about how I run my business, without you questioning my life choices, so just drop it, okay?"

An uneasy silence fills the wood-paneled box as we

continue our ascent. I stare straight ahead at the doors, not even wanting to look at Pettibone. He clears his throat and starts to talk again.

"I believe we may have gotten off on the wrong foot," he says quietly. "I never meant to cause any offense, sir. If Mistress Ziva has faith in you, then so do I."

A sigh escapes my lips, and I relent in my dislike of the guy, but only slightly.

"No problem, shorty," I say absently. He huffs lightly beside me.

"I do wish you wouldn't call me that," he says. "Or any other epithet about my height. It is most undignified."

"I guess that makes us even, then," I remark, a crooked smile on my face.

"Perhaps," Pettibone sighs, cleaning his spectacles with a cloth. He puts them back on his muzzle and turns to me.

"I am not your enemy, Mr. Llewellyn," he says. "But I must impress upon you the gravity of the situation. As you have surmised, Mistress Ziva and her family are highly regarded, not only among the nobility of the Zebra Nation but also in Newland's politics. Mistress Ayani's disappearance, if made public, could spell ruin for the family in both capacities. I daren't even mention the irreparable damage to the progress of Newland-Zebra Nation diplomacy."

My head spins a little, with the sheer number of fancy words this guy's throwing around, but I get the gist of what he's saying. I really do need to keep this on the low-down, or else, not only does my contract dry up, but so do a lot of other things. I simply nod to him in agreement and realize that my previously drunken, scathing remarks might have had a kernel of truth in them. I acknowledge his concern, and we spend the rest of the ride up in silence.

* * *

A bell rings, and the doors open. Penthouse. This must be it. There's a long, wide corridor in front of us, the walls once again lined with traditional, abstract paintings from the Nation, of hunting scenes and tribal dances, at least as far as I can figure. Also filed along the corridor are more guards, most of them carrying spears, but more than a few carrying automatic weapons. I guess they take the security of their diplomats very seriously. They're all looking straight ahead, soundless, raising their weapons quietly to attention as we pass.

"Who are these guys?" I murmur to Pettibone.

"The Ashk'ari," he says, passively. "The traditional ceremonial guard of the Zebra Nation nobility."

"Are they always this quiet?" I say, feeling more and more creeped out by the guards' silence.

"Of course," Pettibone replies like it's the most normal thing in the world. "They are bound by a vow of silence. A useful trait for the deadliest hunters and warriors of the Zebra Nation."

That statement does nothing to ease the tension I'm feeling, only magnifying it to excruciating levels. I'm afraid that if I put a toe out of line, I'll be set upon by some of the most highly trained killers this side of the Holbrook, or this side of the world, for that matter. We continue in relative silence, my longer strides echoing alongside the short, measured pace of Pettibone. Finally, after what seems like an eternity, we reach the huge double doors leading to what I'm guessing is the Ambassadorial suite of rooms belonging to Ziva and her family.

158

"Wait here," says Pettibone before quietly slipping in through the door. I wait, really wishing I could smoke in here, listening intently but not wanting to incur the wrath of the Ashk'ari. Less than a minute passes before he reappears.

"Mistress Onyelé will see you now," he says primly, and he ushers me inside.

The tension seems to leave almost immediately. The room before me is opulent, with many plush sofas and armchairs and ornately designed rugs clustering around an unlit fireplace. To one side stands a liquor cabinet, a delicate crystal decanter and glasses standing on a' sideboard next to it, almost teasing. A chandelier hangs from the ceiling, illuminating the whole scene with countless iridescent flecks, softer than the harsh light of the hallway. The scent of furniture polish and incense hangs heavily in the air, along with that zebra smell, and a gold carriage clock proudly stands on the mantelpiece, the hands reading seven thirty precisely. I guess Pettibone is nothing if not anally punctual. Ziva is sitting in one of the voluptuous armchairs, her face weary, dressed much as she had been when she first came calling on me, just in a different color, a vivid blue this time. Pettibone turns sharply on his heel and addresses his mistress.

"Will that be all, Mistress Ziva?" He asks courteously.

"Yes, thank you, Clarence. That will be all," she says before he smartly swishes past me and back out into the hall, closing the doors quietly behind him.

Butler, huh? Ziva turns to me. If the natural black stripes of her skin didn't run under her tired, bloodshot eyes, I'd swear there were dark circles there. She probably hasn't been getting too much sleep lately, and I don't blame her. There's a moment of silence as she motions for me to sit across from her, and I oblige, laying my hat on the table between us. It's a business thing, laying your hat across from your client. Makes them feel more comfortable. I look around, trying to see if there's an ashtray around that I can use.

"Mind if I smoke?" I ask her, and she nods.

"Go ahead," she replies. "I have asked the staff to make provision for you."

She slides a small, cut crystal ashtray across the table. It probably costs more than my apartment building, so I delicately accept it and search around in my pockets for my cigarettes. I find one and light up just before Ziva asks me the question I've been waiting for.

"So," she begins. "What have you found out so far?"

I take a thoughtful drag on the smoke, formulating a response. It's probably best if I'm straight with her. No use offering false hope.

"I haven't found her yet, if that's what you mean," I say. "But I have found plenty of evidence connected to some sort of trouble she might be in."

"Trouble?" Ziva asks, a look of worry and confusion spreading over her face. "What trouble?"

"Trouble that may go further than I can tell you," I reply, taking another drag to keep calm. "Seems your sister disappeared of her own volition. She doesn't want to be found."

"That's impossible," Ziva says. "What can she find out there in this horrible city when she has everything here?"

"Freedom…" I say, tapping off a length of ash and trying not to get offended. "A chance to be her own animal, without someone looking over her shoulder and judging her every move. I'm guessing she's the rebellious kind."

It's not so much a question as it is a statement of fact, but Ziva looks sullenly at me and nods all the same. Seems my assumption was correct. She sighs and stares into the unlit fireplace, and I carefully stub out the cigarette. It's then that I notice that it's a gas fire, and a lower-end one at that. In fact, now that the initial awe of being inside the embassy has worn off, everything around me seems to have a more worn, cheap look to it: the furniture, the table, even the clock on the imitation marble mantelpiece. Something about that strikes me as odd. Does the Zebra Nation really pay and look after its representatives so poorly? I push the thought to the back of my mind as Ziva speaks again.

"You are correct, Mr. Llewellyn," she says. "My sister has always been a wandering spirit. It has caused our father no end of heartache, the way she carries on. He has tried his best to discipline her properly, but I fear it has not been enough."

"And your mother?" I ask.

"She rests with the ancestors," says Ziva quietly. I get the picture.

"Sorry," I say. "Thoughtless of me."

"It is quite all right, Mr. Llewellyn," she says. "It was many years ago. But come now, what do you have there?"

She points to the package I'm carrying, and I look down at it. I guess the moment is finally here to show her what I've found. I produce the brown paper bag from under my arm and remove the sterilized, clear plastic bag from inside it, the one containing the blood-stained clothing. It's a shock to Ziva. She claps her hands to her mouth in disbelief as I gently place my findings on the table and slide them across to her. The initial effect wears off quickly, and a confused look passes over Ziva's features.

"This must be wrong," she says incredulously. "I know my sister. Ayani would not be caught dead in something like this!"

"Not as well as you might think," I retort. "And she was seen very much alive when she last wore these. Like you said, wandering spirit."

"There must be some mistake!" Ziva screams at me indignantly. I remain calm. I know exactly where these came from and the circumstances, but I'll need Ziva's cooperation to prove my theory. I take in a deep breath and prepare to ask a question that will leave no room for doubt.

"What size does your sister wear?" I ask.

"What sort of question is that?" Ziva replies, the ire clear in her voice.

"Just answer the question, please; it will help," I ask, very reasonably. Although she's still agitated, Ziva answers by saying that her sister is a size eight. I smile inwardly, but I don't let the expression cross my face. I invite Ziva to check the clothes, and she does so, peering through the clear bag at the laundry tags. Size eight. Another look of disbelief from Ziva. I light another smoke. I'm on a roll.

"These could be anyone's..." she says, her voice shaking. Time to bring out the big guns. Something irrefutable. I reach into the bag for the coin purse and pass it to her.

"I found this with it, too," I say, the cigarette dangling from my lips. "I think you'll recognize it, and the contents."

Recognition does dawn in Ziva's eyes, alongside a growing level of anxiety, so much so that I can smell it on her. She opens the purse and immediately finds Ayani's I.D. card. She sits quietly, her eyes fixed on the card in her hand, motionless, though her fingers quiver with fear. I take another drag on the cigarette, feeling genuinely concerned for my client, before exhaling a small cloud of smoke. It's so still in the room that I can hear the faint ticking of the clock, the distant groan of traffic beyond the windows, and the quiet, furtive shuffling of the Ashk'ari guards just outside the door. I need to say something.

"I found them in a dumpster behind a strip club in Coldwater," I say. Ziva remains as impassive as a statue, still fixated on the I.D. I sigh, remembering the awful scene I'd witnessed and everything I'd discovered over the past few days.

"Not sure if you've been following the papers, but there was a fight," I continue. "Lots of animals died there. That's the reason for the blood."

Ziva's head snaps to attention, now focused on me, panic welling up from deep inside her, flowing from her like a fountain.

"Was she...?" Ziva asks, but I quickly cut in, having anticipated the question.

"No, she's alive," I say. "As far as I can tell. She got away."

"How can you be sure?" she asks. I simply tap the side of my nose.

"The old sniffer hasn't steered me wrong yet," I say, taking pride in my words. "Though it has been misled a couple of times over the past few days. But I'm convinced your sister is alive and still in Oldsburg."

Ziva gives a sigh of relief, possibly the first one she's had in weeks, before putting the card back in the purse. I stub out the cigarette, the last dying embers still producing a minute stream of grey-white smoke. I don't share in her relief as I

163

reach for the note that I got from Hank's belongings, but I think better of it. I don't want to worry my client any further.

"At least she still has her Spirit Key..." she says quietly, and a knot of dread forms in my gut.

"Uh... about that..." I say uncomfortably. Ziva's eyes widen, and she frantically checks the purse again, finding the little sliver of wood with its peeling yellow paint. She plucks it deftly from its hiding place and holds it like one of the Sainted clutching their Rosary.

"My sister is in grave danger..." she says quietly. "She has been separated from her ancestors..."

I cock an eyebrow at this, but Ziva's genuine concern also stirs a well of curiosity. From what I could gather, the whole Spirit Key thing was a load of superstitious bunk, nothing a well-educated zebra would hold to. Seems that notion is untrue. I hunch forward in the chair to continue speaking, but Ziva is already up and hurrying towards me like Old Scratch himself is nipping at her heels.

"You have to go!" she says, a terrified urgency in her words. "Quickly! You have to find her!"

I get up, unbelieving, while she bustles past me to the door, and I follow along, my ear twitching as I put my beaten-up old fedora back on my head. Ziva opens the door abruptly, and I can see she's trembling. I raise my bandaged hand, intending to pat her on the shoulder reassuringly, but I think better of it. She smells of fear, that sour smell that I've encountered far too often in my life. I sigh and think of the words that need to be said.

"Listen," I say to her. "You can keep hold of Ayani's belongings for now, but if it comes to getting the police involved, I'm going to need them back. Chain of evidence and all that. You know where I am; just send them along if I need them."

"Yes, yes, very well, just go!" She says hurriedly, before pushing me through the door and slamming it behind me. The sound rumbles down the empty hallway like a cannon blast, and a dozen pairs of mute eyes stare at me briefly before going back to staring straight ahead. I make my way towards the elevator, press the button, and think about what I'm going to do next.

I'm back in my apartment by half nine, and the building is mercifully quiet for once, without the usual sounds of the raucous parties that Eduardo throws on what seems like a nightly basis. I lock the door behind me and put the chain on, right before slouching to my office and slumping into my chair. I don't know what Ziva expects; detective work takes time, which is something she isn't giving me. Finding her sister's Spirit Key really spooked her, though I didn't expect it to be to that extent. I still think it's a lot of hokum, but then again, a lot of people, myself included, take a lot of comfort in the Saints, and they're just as intangible as these ancestors and spirits that the zebras believe in. Different strokes for different folks, I guess. I push the thought out of my mind and reach for the whiskey on my desk before thinking better of it. I know I really need to cut down. I sigh, irritated, and stand up, grabbing the pack of smokes from my pocket and going to my record player. Jazz always helps me think better, especially if it's more downbeat. I shuffle through my collection of LPs and decide on the Joe Wilson Ensemble. I scan my eyes down the sleeve and pick a tune I like, placing the vinyl delicately on the platter before dropping the needle. Soon enough, just after the scratchy hiss of the recording starts, the soft sounds of the blues fill the room.

I need to check my notes again. Recap and go back to basics. There's got to be something I'm missing; I just know it. I rifle through the pages of my notebook, checking every clue and conversation I've had over the last few days, looking for any inconsistencies or contradictions. I barely even register that I still have an unlit cigarette in my mouth, the filter gradually going soggy. I light up, frustrated, and take a long drag. The rush of nicotine calms my frayed nerves a little, but I'm still determined to find something. I don't know what I'm looking for, but I'll know what it is when I see it. My eyes feel dry as I continue to read my hastily (and, in some cases, sloppily) scribbled notes. I keep puffing on the smoke, almost burning it down to the filter before I realize it. All the evidence is right there in front of me, but it still doesn't make any sense. I light another cigarette, not even caring that I'm chain-smoking, and rub my eyes with the heel of my good hand, trying to stave off the inevitable march of fatigue.

Let's see... Benny checks out, though his statement is a little superfluous to the current situation. Hank's address book is another dead end. Ziva and Pettibone have been as good as useless so far, other than character reference. My escapade with Ramona had given me a little food for thought, though I still can't see what connects Daniel Arden to Ayani Onyelé, other than that they were in the same place at the wrong time, and some vague connections to the Donati pack. The letter which was meant to be given to Ayani, while threatening, doesn't really give me much to work with other than the scent of a Doberman and sea salt. It's pretty obvious they're after her, but what for? Money? It can't be that. Ayani's family, despite their diplomatic ties, don't seem especially loaded. There must be some other reason behind the threats.

A thought occurs to me. It's more than possible that the Donati pack were after Daniel Arden as well, and that makes a lot more sense. The Arden Shipping Company is a multi-million-dollar business, and they'd probably pay anything to get one of the noble scions of Conroy back. But, with Danny dead, maybe the pack is looking for another target? If that's the case, then maybe Leo Donati is getting rusty in his old age. I sigh once again, more defeated than frustrated. What am I *missing*? The cloud of sleep is already creeping up on me as I glance drowsily towards the clock on the wall. It's nearly two a.m. I lean back in my chair and quietly drift to sleep, accompanied by the white-noise hiss of the record spinning fruitlessly on the turntable.

I'm running. At least, I think I am. It's hard to move my legs or get any air into my lungs. The darkness is all around me, reaching for me with tendril fingers. The maddening whispers and snippets of conversation dart past my ears on the cloying breeze. What are they saying? Mocking laughter rolls by like thunder, just as fleeting, but twice as aggressive. What do they want from me? What do they want me to do? The whispers louden into muttered curses and doubts. Am I really up to this job? Am I past my prime? Too old and fat and dumb to solve this?

A shaft of light pierces the suffocating blackness. I dive towards it, but something snags my foot, cold and tense. I try to shake loose, but the force just pulls harder. The laughter returns, but this time I can tell whose voice it is. It's Tilton.

I lash out with my other foot, somehow causing the awful

grip to slacken. The momentum pushes me toward the light, and I streak towards it like a comet. The beacon grows closer. I can almost taste it.

I wake, bleary-eyed and with a nicotine headache. I rub my temples with a weary finger and look up at the clock. It's just after nine in the morning, and I can hear the record player still hissing like an angry snake, strangely louder than the usual Oldsburg traffic beyond my window. I shake my head to get rid of the last threads of sleep before going to the player and lifting the needle from the vinyl. I carefully put the disc back in its sleeve and return to my chair, once again staring at my accumulated notes like something is going to suddenly jump out at me. I pour myself a glass of bourbon and sip at it, scanning everything in front of me.

Threatening letter, check. Notebook, double-check. Address book… wait a minute… there could be something more in there. I mean, I only skimmed it last time. Maybe a more thorough examination is necessary? With Ayani being a runaway, she probably wouldn't have the funds readily to hand to afford somewhere to stay. If my hunch holds, she's probably crashing with a co-worker, likely female. I run through all the names and addresses listed in the book, but it becomes apparent very quickly that I need to narrow the search area.

I pull out a roadmap of Oldsburg and a pencil. My instinct tells me to stick to this side of the river, and most likely around the Coldwater district and the immediately surrounding areas. That scratches a lot of names from the list, all stage names like Candy, Lexi, and at least three Sapphires. Hank has also helpfully noted the species of each of the workers alongside their names and addresses. Going over the list again, I don't see any bats, which rules out her staying in the Hollows. Easttown is an industrial area so that just leaves the Bowery, Coldwater, Cheapside, and the Pastures. It's still a lot of ground to cover, so I start striking more names in a methodical manner. Coldwater would be too close to make a clean getaway, and it's the main turf of the packs, so that district is out. My search leads further north, the net gradually tightening.

I light my last cigarette and draw the smoke into my lungs, coughing slightly at how dry my throat is. I get up and start pacing slowly, staring at the map, now covered in pencil marks. The Pastures is too far away. I move back to my desk and cross out the names with addresses in that neighborhood. That just leaves the Bowery and Cheapside. Going back over the list of names for what seems like the hundredth time, one sticks out like a sore thumb: Amber. Seems she has an apartment nearby. Something gets my dander up. I try to remember back to the start of the investigation and her statement. She never mentioned what she did after everything happened, and she said that she hadn't seen Ayani among the bodies. That didn't mean she hadn't seen her alive... a grim smile crosses my face.

My intuition tells me that Ayani must be staying with Amber. I allow myself a little, satisfied grin, though it's not a pleasant one, and I suddenly realize what day it is. I check the clock on my wall. It's coming up to noon. Have I really spent nearly three hours at this? The boys from the precinct will be gathering at Sam's in about an hour to pay respects to Boscoe on the anniversary of his death. A pang of guilt runs through me. As much as I don't want to, I really should go. I'll probably be the only person there who really knew him. I guess Amber can wait a couple of hours. She's probably not going anywhere.

With a sigh, I change into my more respectable black suit before heading out the door. There's something I have to do first.

The Lister Cemetery on the west side of the river is where Boscoe was buried. I remember it all too well. I was there when they shoveled in the first clods of dirt. Commissioner Talbot gave a stirring eulogy that day, which didn't surprise me; he was always a good orator. What did surprise me at the time was just how many members of the department attended that funeral. Beyond that, I don't remember much, mainly because I was drowning my sorrows for at least a few days afterward, if not a week. Good thing I'd got a lot of leave saved up. That was a bad episode in my life, what with one thing and another.

I kneel and lay the bottle of whiskey on Boscoe's grave, the brown paper it's wrapped in rustling against glass and stone. I still remember his brand, even after so long. It's Green Tail, a brand from the Emeralds that he remembered from his youth and from his ancestry. It's strange how quiet everything can be in a graveyard, all the noise and ruckus muted out by the dead. I take a deep breath, letting it rattle out of me. There's a saying in the department that your partner is closer to you than your wife. Anything you can't tell your wife, you tell your partner. I suppose the sense of bereavement can be just as acute.

"I'm sorry, Boscoe," I say to the tombstone. "You were always there for me, but I wasn't there for you. Best I can do is give an offering…"

It's the only offering there so far. No other wreaths or charms or anything. The silence pervades every inch of the graveyard and my own being. I hear a raven caw in the still air, one of those that hadn't been Awakened and just stayed a simple beast. I push that thought to the back of my mind, how my ancient ancestors were some of the lucky ones. All that matters is me and the stone. I clear my throat, the sound cracking through the air like a gunshot. That one fateful gunshot.

"I'm cutting down," I say, feeling guilty for the mistruth of it, "and... and..."

I'm trying to find the words, but they just stick in my throat. What can I say? This guy was like a mentor and older brother to me. Mere words would do him a disservice. I just sigh again, like it will calm me down. The wind rustles through the trees, bringing with it the scent of old, dead things... and a familiar, artisan perfume.

"Hello, Jen," I say. I'd recognize the smell anywhere. Jennifer Cassidy is right behind me. She leans forward, placing a wreath beside the bottle, the flowers — poppies — a vibrant yellow compared to the dull green of the grass and the drab grey of the stone. Yellow poppies were always Boscoe's favorite flower, and I'm not sure how I remember that, or how Jen remembered that.

"Hello, Rex," she says solemnly. "Seems we're the only ones who even remember where Boscoe is buried, huh? Need a hand up?"

She extends a slender hand to me, wrapped up in a black satin opera glove. I graciously accept and try to stand, my knees creaking like old timbers with the effort. After brushing the dust from my legs, I turn to Jen. She's dressed up to the

171

nines, not just with the opera gloves, but a black satin dress, black high heels, and a black fur stole (imitation, of course). On her head is a black fascinator with a black veil. Next to me, she looks like a movie star in mourning. I don't smile, and neither does she. I suppose that's the effect graveyards can have on people, sapping the joy from you, especially when you're visiting an old friend.

"Good to see you," I say to her. "Going to Sam's?"

"I am," she replies. "It's only right. Boscoe was my friend too, you know."

I do know. In fact, it was Boscoe who first introduced us, though how he knew Jen was — and will forever remain — a mystery to me. That's the thing about Jen; she's always been secretive about her past, even with me.

"I know," I say absently. "I just hope you're ready for an evening with Oldsburg's biggest boy's club."

"Still no ladies on the force, huh?" She says, cocking an eyebrow,

"Not as far as I know, Jen," I reply.

We start walking back towards the cemetery gates, my hands in my pockets, one of hers clutching a black purse, the other around my shoulders. She almost seems to glide like a ghost, which is pretty eerie given our surroundings. The only sounds that stand out are the clack of her heels on the path and the distant murmur of the omnipresent Oldsburg traffic.

"There have to be some females in the department, surely?" She finally says, breaking the awkward quiet. "I saw a few the other day when I met you at the Fourth."

"Met isn't the word I'd use, Jen," I say, a crack of a smile on my lips. "Saved is more like it!"

At this, she lets out a stifled laugh, trying to respect the solemnity of the place and failing. Seems she found it as humorous as I did.

"As for women in the department," I continue. "Yeah, there are a lot of meter-maids, and desk-types, and a few who give support on cases with kids or beaten wives, but none on the street."

"I guess some things in Oldsburg never change," Jen sighs.

"Yeah... I guess so..." I trail off.

We make our way to Sam's via the subway, crossing the Holbrook from Lister. The place is like an institution among Oldsburg's cops, one of the few bars that's frequented almost entirely by officers and their families, whether retired or still working. As such, even though it's situated in the lower rent district of Cheapside, there's virtually no trouble. Who in their right mind would want to mess with a bar full of liquored-up policemen, many of whom carry guns even when off duty? Not to mention Sam himself, a grizzled old bloodhound who, after retiring from the force, set up a safe haven for any cop wanting a good, stiff drink? I knew the dog from before he retired, and he was one of the toughest and most honest cops I ever met, despite being on the vice squad for his obvious talents at sniffing out evidence.

The place is usually quiet, too, but it seems that's untrue today. The whole taproom is packed with officers of all species; the older, retired generation who knew Boscoe as a cadet, all in their civvies, rubbing shoulders with many more my age, and more than a few rookies who probably have no real right being here. A lot of the congregation are in uniform, fresh off morning patrol. Sam is on bar, and right behind him, next to the neon green lights and promotional plates, is a framed black-and-white photograph of Boscoe in his prime.

A sudden sense of discomfort seeps into my chest. Tilton was right; I shouldn't be here. I'm probably the only animal in the room who was let go, rather than retiring at the right age, along with... I feel Jen put a comforting hand on my arm, and the doubt seems to evaporate. Among the press of animals, I see Tony Henderson at the bar in his ostentatious dress uniform, all commendations and ribbons and jingle-bell medals, his pop-bottle glasses grotesquely magnifying his eyes as he regales a group of younger officers with some joke or story. A bout of uproarious laughter rings out among the gathering before Tony notices me and waves both me and Jen over with his trademark wide, welcoming smile. I look to Jen, and she nods with a smile of her own, so we move to stand by the old terrier. I proffer my left hand, and he shakes it in a firm but friendly manner.

"Rex, my boy, good to see you!" Tony says with genuine enthusiasm. A few bewildered glances pass between the younger officers around us, one of whom I remember as the crane from the front desk only a few days ago, the one with his beak in a comic book. I shrug modestly.

"Let me get you a drink," Tony says, and I don't gainsay him. Soon enough, there's a glass of beer in my hand, and Tony is singing my praises like I'm the second coming, or at least near enough.

"This guy here," Tony starts. "Was Boscoe's partner for years! One of the best officers on the force! Even stood up to old Commissioner Radcliffe more than once!"

A gallery of vacant stares greets that statement. These guys are too young to know who Radcliffe was. Besides, I'm not too happy having my past exposed before everyone, especially if it has to do with the department. My cheeks are already flushing red, hidden by the fur on my face. From among the throng of rookies, I hear a plaintive call.

"Who?"

So that's who I am among the boys, huh? Just a footnote to be forgotten. My nerves are getting frayed. I really don't want to be here, but with Tony on one arm, and Jen on the other, I can't exactly bolt for the door.

"Are you all right, Rex?" I hear in my ear. It's Jen.

That tears it. I ignore her and head further down the long bar, not even caring that her hand has slipped from my arm. I just shove the beer glass into some nameless cadet's hand as I pass, probably making his afternoon. I'm not in the mood for sympathy or empathy. I order a double bourbon before my eye catches an older face further down the bar, almost squeezed into the corner while a lot of the younger guys shoot pool nearby. I recognize the face, but the name eludes me like a fleeting shadow. I guess that's the way things get as you grow older and more distant from the people you once knew.

I don't even pay for the drink, just staring sullenly into the amber liquid, my collar and tie feeling uncomfortably hot and choking. Sam usually just chalks up what I owe him on my tab, the one I've gradually been running up and paying off since I was with the department. I'll pay it all back to him someday, I'm sure, but not today. I pick up the glass and sip at it. It's my favorite brand — Jerry Wingate's Old No. 5. It's expensive but worth every cent. Aged in old champagne casks, it goes down as smooth as silk and as mellow as a summer evening. I don't get it that often because it's so pricy, usually settling for Oscar Webb Blue Label whenever I hit up the convenience store on my block. I also didn't ask for it by name, but I guess the department is footing the bill, so Sam is probably going to be generous with what he serves, especially to people he's known for a good twenty years or more.

Jen has made her way to me, the mass of males parting before her like wheat before a scythe, and just as speechless. She leans her elbows on the bar beside me, which accentuates her hips. She's probably loving the attention, with more than a few catcalls and wolf-whistles behind her, some of which actually come from the lips of cats and wolves. I try to ignore them, just continuing to sip from my glass and avoid eye contact with anyone.

"What's up, Rex?" She asks like she can't tell.

"You know what's up," I reply curtly. "I shouldn't be here. This isn't my scene."

"It's more your scene than these little boys playing copper," she replies blithely, showing absolutely no respect for the young rookie officers around us. It rankles me a little, but I silently agree with her.

"Besides," she continues. "You've got more right than anyone, to be here. You were Boscoe's partner. That should count for something, right?"

Once again, in my mind, I agree with her, but I show no outward expression of it, apart from possibly pausing with the glass of bourbon to my lips. I sigh quietly. I know she's right, as always. I guess that's what makes her a decent reporter; she can read people better than most and cut right to the heart of the issue at hand. So why does it irk me so? A martini slides down the bar, coming to rest precisely in front of Jen, with not a drop of liquid spilling. It's an impressive feat, given that it's in a cocktail glass. Seems Sam is still in practice at slinging drinks accurately. I look to Jen, who picks up the glass daintily and holds it toward me.

"Well, as my daddy always used to say," she says, smiling. "If you can't lick 'em, join 'em."

I smile too, touching glasses with hers, the light chink almost lost among the crowd of voices and laughter behind us.

"I'll drink to that," I say, sipping at the Old No. 5 again. Things might not be so bad after all.

It seems I was right. Things haven't turned out too bad so far. Apart from dodging Tilton and Bose at every step, Jen and I have had a swell time. I can't remember how many shots of bourbon I've had, but I'm starting to feel a little giddy. It also certainly helps that I've run into some familiar faces that I can put names to other than Tony, people I can actually shoot the breeze with about the old days. I've had a good conversation with Archie Mendoza, a beaver who's not much older than I am. We swap pleasantries, catching up on family and so on. Seems his two brothers are still in the construction business, like a lot of beavers, and his oldest son is just starting middle school. Hawley Edwards, an aging panther who used to be Mendoza's partner, quickly joins the conversation, and it's like I'd never left the department. We discuss old cases, memorable moments, and a few somber reflections on Boscoe. We all raise a glass to his memory, privately, before getting back to enjoying ourselves.

However, as the afternoon drags on into evening, and more and more animals come and go as shifts start and finish, I find myself alone with Jen once more. I can't be sure, but I don't think she's had more than a couple of drinks all day, despite the many offers she's had from various animals, all of which she has graciously declined. Looking out for me, maybe? I don't know, but if that's true, I appreciate the thought. The room has mostly cleared now, with only the really heavy drinkers and assorted hangers-on still around from the initial gathering. The sun has set, and despite my initial misgivings, I'm having a good time.

Or, at least, I *was* having a good time. Tilton and a gaggle of his vice squad underlings sit at a table near us, the fat hog laughing uproariously at something or other, followed by the high-pitched cackling of that crummy hyena, Bose. This is usually followed by guffaws and chuckles from the rest of Tilton's crew, all either too dumb or too frightened of the slob to say anything against him. I know it's none of my business, but I prick up my ears and try to find out what's so damn funny. They're talking about Boscoe.

"I'm not sayin' Boscoe was a bad guy, Saints rest his soul," Tilton says, a little too loudly. "But he din't know what wuz good for 'im."

My hackles rise at the implication, but it seems Tilton hasn't noticed who's sitting only a few tables away from him. One voice agrees with him, the sneering voice of Bose, adding more fuel to the fire.

"Yeah, he wasn't what you'd call smart," the hyena drawls, in the most energized yet lazy tone of voice. "Didn't even try giving the wrongly accused the benefit of the doubt."

He didn't take bribes from packsters and vigilance crews, you mean? My good hand clenches into a fist, and Jen seems to notice. Looks like her hearing is as good as mine because she's put a warning hand on my arm, her fingers tightening but never saying a word. I ease up a little in my impotent rage. What does Bose's opinion really matter to me? I know the guy's a thug, a crook who somehow managed to worm his way into a uniform, but it's not like he's in any position of real authority. He's not likely to sway junior officers, but there's someone at that table who is.

"A total hard-ass," Tilton adds, grunting as he chugs a beer. "No sense o' humor. Always pickin' on those he thought wuz beneath 'im."

My thoughts tumble around at those words. *Maybe that's because you hated him, you slob*, I think to myself, *and for good reason.* He was wise to Tilton's shenanigans since that pig was a cadet. I know the name of the anonymous whistle-blower who had Tilton up for more disciplinary hearings than you can count. How did he ever get through them all, with little more than docked pay? My thoughts drift back to Commissioner Radcliffe, and the connection is clear. And when the hell will that hog ever learn to shut up? My angry, spiteful thoughts are interrupted by what Tilton says next, and an icy chill, runs through my gut.

"An' another thing, I heard his ol' partner, Rex Llewellyn, got him killed," he says conspiratorially. "Walked right into an ambush 'cuz Llewellyn wasn't watchin' his back. Blown ta shreds, they say."

The pain of the memory kicks me in the chest like a steer. I remember every detail, and it's not what Tilton is describing at all. There was no ambush. We'd just replied to a call of suspicious activity and wound up fighting for our lives when things went south. Rather than feeling ashamed or sad or pained by it, I just feel angry. More than angry; enraged.

"Ya know," Tilton continues. "I hear Llewellyn is here tonight. I dunno how he even dares show 'is face here at all, after whut he did."

179

Jen's fingers tighten even more on my arm as I bare my teeth in anger, like a death-grip, trying to keep me from doing something I'll regret, but I don't care. I furiously shake free of her grasp and stand up. The only things I see in the room are Tilton and me, and I march right over to the stupid pig as he's raising a toast, the blood pounding in my ears, his words reaching my brain like they were trudging through molasses.

"To Boscoe," the words echo. "The dumbest good cop in Oldsburg! Rest in peace and bless you, my son!"

He even has the temerity to imitate Boscoe's way of speaking on that last part. The thunderous anger within me is subsumed into a smoldering blackness that's even more powerful. I was going to bark at him and show him what for, but now… now, he's gone too far. The eyes of Tilton's stooges all converge on me, but I don't care. My mind is calm and clear, my muzzle expressionless. I tap the greasy hog on the shoulder, and he turns to me, his face still cracked in an ugly grin, yellow tusks fully on show. On seeing me, he stands up, almost too quickly, and turns on his used-car-salesman act, all oily, with a distinct effort at being charming and friendly.

"Ey, Llewellyn!" He feigns. "Good t' see ya, buddy! How've ya bin?"

"You on duty?" I ask, coldly,

"Whut?" He asks dumbly. "No, why would I be? I'm here rememberin' a great loss to the departm-"

Before he can finish his sentence, my good hand snaps immediately to his jaw, a clean left hook that I should have given him days ago, the impact barely registering in my mind. The punch catches him totally by surprise, and he spins like a top into the table behind him, slamming into it with most of his weight, glasses and bottles clattering and crashing to the floor. He lies there for a few seconds before I give him a piece of my mind.

"Don't you *ever* talk about Boscoe that way again, you ignorant fucking *swine!*" I bark in my anger, the pounding in my ears subsiding. "You can insult me all you like, but don't you *ever* talk shit about him again!"

A few gasps and murmurs have arisen from the few remaining patrons, with the only other sound being the corny rock music coming from the glass-fronted jukebox that some younger boy must have put on cue before departing, sounding almost tragically distant. Tilton's mob are helping him up, and he's struggling to break free of them and land one back on me, but even he's not strong enough that six guys can't hold him. I turn and walk away, heading for the door like I'm on casters. I absently tell Sam I'll pay for the damages, but he brushes it off, saying something about the department paying for it, right before he scowls at Tilton. Jen hurries along after me, her heels clacking along the tiled floor and then the wood floor. I feel like I'm floating on air, and not in a good way. This is the kind of air where you need a parachute, otherwise it's sidewalk-pizza time. Tilton is still raging and swearing incoherently behind me, but as I open the door and the chilly evening breeze hits me, I hear a few words.

"Don't worry about him, Mark," says Bose. "He's just a washed-up old drunk. Not worth your time."

I pause briefly, the words stabbing into me just as harshly as what had come before. But I'm the bigger animal in this. I simply walk away.

As I'm walking from Sam's back to my place, I stop to ponder what I just did. Will Tilton press charges, or will his lackeys convince him that I'm not worth the time? Whatever the outcome, he'll probably hold a grudge. That's just the kind of animal he is, stubborn and mean. Jen hasn't caught up with me yet. She's probably smoothing things over back at the bar, not that it matters. Sam was definitely on my side in that little disagreement. I guess that old dog's loyalty is hard-earned, and I've earned it. Jen is probably also sweet-talking Tilton into being a good boy. She's the only creature on this planet that can get the guy to behave.

I lean against a lamppost, the spring night-mist creeping around my ankles, and reach into my pocket for a cigarette. Sam has a no smoking policy in his bar, probably because of his own sensitive bloodhound nose, and I can appreciate that, so I've been craving this one for a while now. I put it between my lips and spark my lighter, the moisture in the air forming a pleasing halo around the flame. I touch the fire to the paper and breathe in. The heady mixture of the night air, the smoke, and the copious amount of booze I've consumed in the last few hours makes my head swim, but not unpleasantly.

I sort of feel like a weight has been lifted from my shoulders by decking Tilton, but I can't be sure if it really has. Was I really so green as to let Boscoe get killed? Was it an accident, or was it my rookie mistake? The seeds of doubt start to germinate once again in my mind, and I hang my head to think. Why can't I let go? Why must I keep torturing myself about Boscoe?

It's just at this point — at one of my worst moments of self-doubt — that Jen finally catches up with me. She's not flustered, not red around the ears like her breed can be when they've been exerting themselves. It seems like she's been following me in a leisurely fashion. She also has a kind of smug, triumphant look on her face, like she's bested someone in a challenge of wits. My guess is that she has everything under control, which is just like her.

"Marcus won't be causing you any fuss," she smiles at me in a devilish fashion. "Not if he wants to keep his little... indiscretions out of the paper."

"And you believe him?" I ask, exhaling a puff of smoke,

"Trust me, I've got more dirt on him than he realizes," she says with a wink. "He won't go back on his word. I guarantee it."

I breathe a small sigh of relief. I don't exactly want to end up in the pound or have my license revoked for slugging a detective in the vice squad, even if he was off duty and deserved to get punched. I slowly start to feel the ache in my knuckles from the hit. That guy's got a granite jaw and virtually no scruples. It's small wonder he's gone far in vice. I turn to Jen, the lamplight illuminating her features and the evening mist playing around them.

"Thanks, Jen," I simply say before taking another drag on my smoke.

"No need to thank me," she replies casually. "But you do seem troubled. More than usual, I mean."

She's right once more, of course. Everything that's happened to me over the last few days has tended to rattle me. The weird coincidences, getting drugged, being hit on by someone half my age, the case being put under pressure from my client, and my sense of not really belonging with my old colleagues anymore. Not to mention the fact that I've been goofing off my responsibilities to the case because of sentimentality. Then Tilton starts really strumming on my last nerve at Sam's. It snaps, and so do I. It's always been the case that I've wanted to put that pig's lights out, but even so, a remembrance party for Boscoe was exactly the wrong place to do it. I just say nothing and continue smoking.

"What happened to you, Rex?" she asks. "To us? We used to have such fun. Don't you remember?"

"We've changed, Jen," I say to her, flicking the stub of my cigarette into a nearby puddle of water, the end hissing as it fizzles out. "This is my life now, just another shamus. The fun's over."

"How can you be so cold to me, Rex? After all we were to each other," she says, wrapping her fingers around me, pulling me in for a kiss. There, under the glare of an Oldsburg streetlight, our lips meet, electrifying me just like the first time. All the pains and aches in my body that have accumulated over the years just melt away, forgotten in the sweet embrace of this one beautiful creature. However, I taste a tang of want and loneliness on Jen's lips, a hollow void that I can't quite understand. We part lips, and Jen looks to me with her almond-shaped, mahogany-hued eyes.

"Why are we like this, Rex?" she says, trying to sound resolute, holding back tears. "We both know we're no good for each other."

She falls into my arms, though she's a good few inches taller than me. It's a strange sight, to be sure. Fortunately, there's nobody to behold us in our vulnerable, emotional state. I can already feel my heart beginning to beat again. She raises a tear-stained cheek to my ear and whispers, her breath tickling my fur.

"Rex... can I come back to your place? Just until tomorrow morning? Like old times?"

Wait... I've fallen for this line from her before. I'm not

going to let it happen again. I refuse to be hurt again.

"No, you can't. It was you left me, remember?" I say to her, a steely edge creeping into my words. "Back in those old times that you're talking about, you left me two days before we were supposed to be married."

Jen recoils from me, stunned like she's just been stung. She knows I'm right. Your move, Jen.

"I had to think of my career!" she protests. "Tinseltown was the only place I could really shine! And besides, I couldn't get you out of Oldsburg if I had a gun to your head!"

"No, that's true," I say calmly. "I guess a knife to the heart is more direct."

Her eyes harden into slits, and a smirk moves across her face. I knew it was all an act. She was just trying to get close to me, find out what I knew about Ayani. Trying to outpace me. I can't back down from her and relent, not now that I've cottoned on to her ruse. She lets out a short titter of a laugh.

"Ah, same old Rex," she says, almost bemused. "Though it seems you have changed in some ways. You're a lot more hard-hearted, to begin with, and a lot wiser. But never mind. A girl can dream."

"And you've gotten more cunning, sweetheart," I retort. "But it seems the old gags aren't always the best, after all."

"So it would seem," she sighs. "Oh well... guess I'll have to find that story the old-fashioned way."

As she turns to leave, her shoes clattering on the pavement, a thought occurs to me, one that involves a deeply heart-broken young thing propping up the bar at a jazz club across the river. I have to ask her right now or not at all.

"Jen?" I call after her. She pauses in her tracks and turns to me, the gloom softening her outline.

"Yes?" She replies.

"There's this kid, Mary Lansing," I start. "A cat, a student at the U of O. Been hounded by the press for a while now about her late boyfriend. She's at the end of her rope about it. If you're still in good with the editor of the Herald, can you tell him to back off her a bit?"

In the twilight, I can swear that I see a smile cross Jennifer Cassidy's elegant face, probably the first real one she's had since before we left the bar. She thinks on what I've said for a moment before answering.

"Okay, for old times' sake," she finally says. "But that's three you owe me, and you know I'll collect on them eventually. See you 'round, Rexxie-baby."

With nothing more than a swish, a casual wave of her hand, and the sway of her hips, she vanishes into the growing fog. Seems like the old gal still has a soft spot for me after all. I turn and go on my own way, too, accompanied only by my own, ever-present thoughts about the case.

What I don't notice are the four shadowy figures with pointed ears quietly following me as I make my way home.

My steps echo around the almost empty streets as I walk. The evening is wearing on, the dusk looming around every part of Oldsburg's skyline, held back only by the continual glow of the skyscrapers and streetlamps. It's unusually quiet tonight, with only the occasional car coming past, the headlights stabbing through the darkness and fog like a lance before disappearing just as quickly, followed by the thrum of an engine. My guess is that normal animals are having an early night before the daily grind begins afresh tomorrow morning. Then again, I'm not exactly normal as far as occupations go.

My thoughts keep coming back to the case and the potential danger Ayani could be in. Was it really the right call going to Sam's for the day? I'm starting to think it wasn't, given the time constraints I'm under.

As I walk, the gradual fatigue of a full day of drinking starts to bear down on me. My feet start to stagger, but I right myself quickly and redouble my efforts to get home. Maybe I should have called a cab? I dunno. It's not too far to my office, so I might as well save the fare. But at the same time, I really need to get home. To that end, I decide to take a shortcut down an alleyway that cuts out a good portion of my journey. I stop to light a smoke.

I hear the footsteps hurrying up behind me. Too late. In that instant, I realize with horror that I've left my stunner back at the office.

A paw grabs me at the back of my head before I can fully turn it to see what's going on, right before slamming me face-first into the wall at my side. My teeth rattle from the shock, and my worn-out knees crumple like wet cardboard. I land heavily on the ground, then the first wingtip-clad foot thuds into my side, knocking the breath from my lungs. I curl up defensively, but that doesn't stop the rain of kicks and punches that thunder down upon me. My attackers are almost silent, giving only a grunt of exertion every now and then, their fists and feet doing the talking. I risk a glance between my fingers at them, desperately trying to shield my face. Dobermans in suits. They found me. One of the shorter ones barks a command, and they momentarily cease their assault. I feel like I've just had a ton of bricks dropped on me. My ribs are bruised, if not cracked, and I can taste blood in my mouth. The short one orders them to back off, and they obey before they all close in again.

His cronies drag me to my feet, and he presses me against a nearby wall. I don't even notice the transition, but I notice he's a Rottweiler rather than a Doberman. The thick bands of muscle in his arm pin me by the neck, completely helpless. A switchblade materializes in his hand, and I know what he'd like to do with it. As much as I need to keep my cool, this animal could very easily kill me. He hasn't even bared his teeth, and the words come out of him soft and slow, one at a time, from between his grotesquely flapping jowls. He's a professional at intimidation. His black, bottomless eyes pierce into me, every word an agony, especially given the kicking I'd just received.

"Stay. Away. From. Our. Business," he says. "Do you understand me?"

I nod frantically, but those terrible eyes keep staring, not convinced. My own eyes are darting everywhere but his face, almost fit to pop out of my skull, hoping against hope for some miracle. The blade pushes up a little against my neck. He's really not convinced.

"Do you understand me, detective?" He demands. "Do you fucking understand me? Say it!"

I stare into those black, cold pits that should be his eyes, and I see nothing gazing back at me. It's just a dead void — the eyes of a killer. The terrible edge of the steel is pressing uncomfortably against my throat, so I simply nod again, whimpering out a strangled "yes," trying not to accidentally push it into my skin through the fur. That seems to mollify him, he lets me go, and I crumple down into a heap. Through my rapidly bruising eye, I see him turn to his boys.

"Job's done, boys. This dick isn't worth our time," he

says. "Wanna go grab a drink?"

The other dogs agree whole-heartedly to this suggestion like nothing had even happened, completely heedless of the fact that they've just left an animal bruised and bleeding in the gutter. They turn and leave, and after a minute or two, I try getting myself to my feet. My legs falter beneath me again, and I land hard on my backside, desperately hoping the world will stop spinning. My bandaged hand sings a chorus of anguish, the first it's done since I saw Jerome.

I just sit there for a while; tired, beaten, hurting. Was this more than I could handle? I just desperately want to lie down and sleep... No. That's what they'd want me to do, just give up and let them have their way. I can't allow that. I *won't* allow that! I struggle, arching my back against the wall for support, gaining a purchase before propping myself upright. Mad colors dash before my eyes, and I worry about whether those goons have given me a concussion. Shaking my head, the flashes disappear, and I check my chest. Definitely tender, but I'm having no trouble breathing, so nothing's broken. Can't let anybody see me like this. Got to get home. Get home and think.

After what seems like an agonizing trek through the back streets of the Bowery, I finally come upon my little tenement building. Eduardo — St. Roch damn his hide — is having another party. I stagger up the stairs, gripping the handrails, the pain piercing me on every step until I reach my front door. I somehow manage to fumble the keys into the lock, and as soon as the door opens, I as much as collapse over the threshold, the feeling of sleep invading my mind again.

No, got to keep moving. Got to get help. Jerome... No,

won't do to worry him any more than I have to. I've taken worse beatings without him holding my paw. I stumble into my office space, see the bottle of bourbon on my desk, and snatch it up. Then I slouch down. I sit there on the floor, quietly, my back leaning against my desk, Eduardo's damn party heating up just above my head, and unscrew the top of the bottle. I chug back a few deep gulps, wincing at the alcohol, my pains gradually receding with each swig.

They found me and probably know what I'm doing. I don't want to think how. That way lies madness. I touch a finger to the cut on my lip, and the sting tells me it's definitely split. Those guys really did a number on me, but they let me live. Guess they wanted to send a message rather than kill me and have to deal with the inquiries later. The music kicks up a notch in Eduardo's pad, the thumping of music and feet just above me. The driving rhythm only serves to heighten my already turbulent emotions. I'm not afraid of those guys in the packs any more... just angry. Angry and bitter. I take a long draw of the bottle and stand up, swaying from the sudden change.

I need some people who can help me. Bill said to call him if I ever needed him, but I think I'll wait on that a bit. I need to go back to the source: Amber. She knew all along where Ayani was, at least according to my deductions, and yet she didn't say a word, maybe out of fear of someone. Or something. I drink again, just to get my courage to the sticking point, the entire cosmos whirling dizzyingly around me. I succumb and sit heavily at my desk, just to pick up the receiver of my telephone, dialing the number I found in Hank's address book. A cold frustration worries through me as I hear the dial tone, right before an elderly female's voice — possibly

Amber's mother — answers the phone.

"Hello?" She inquires, a worn-out huskiness to her words. "Who is this?"

"Sorry to bother you, ma'am," I start, trying desperately to hide the ire in my tone. "I'm from the Oldsburg PD. I'd like to speak with your daughter?"

"Oh, you mean Racheal?" she says. The name is unfamiliar, but I keep at it.

"Yes, ma'am," I say, trying to sound officious. "Can you get her to the phone? Is she in?"

"No," the old lady replies. "She's with her boyfriend tonight."

Keeping the line open, I quickly grab Hank's address book again and flip to the page detailing Amber's current address. It's incongruous, judging by the area code, but I take a shot anyway.

"Would that be at Apartment 312, Misty Towers, Cheapside?"

"How did you know?" She asks. "Why? Is she in some kind of trouble?"

I don't even bother to answer, just hanging up the receiver. She's confirmed everything, and I don't care if she's calling the actual police station to make sure it was them. I've got my next port of call.

The cab ride could have been a lot smoother, but someone in my present physical state can't exactly choose how the roads are going to be. I patched up a lot of my more superficial wounds before leaving, but my left eye is gradually blackening. I can already feel it puffing up. Wouldn't be surprised if it closes up altogether. My whiskey-driven

191

enthusiasm, along with the time constraints, have taken me to Misty Towers in Cheapside. It's one of those monolithic grey tenement blocks that was built about thirty years ago during the housing crisis, erected cheaply and with plenty of room for as many animals as possible. Nowadays, it's just a run-down wreck of a building, worse than my own, with boarded-up windows to keep the rain out, and every streetlight surrounding it shot out long ago by pushers and pimps, just to keep their dealings secret in a town that, as far as I know, runs on lies and deception.

The front door — a rusted panel, barely hanging from its hinges — isn't even locked, so I let myself in. This is a bad place. I can tell by my nose, no matter how much sour mash I've drunk. There are a whole mess of smells that reek of iniquity: sex, filth, bathtub gin... The echoing cries of the residents don't really help my ears much, either, one apartment blaring some hideous reality show on the tube, another resident scolding their kids, and countless other ear-splitting sounds of misery and hopelessness. I know I should intervene in some of these, but it's not my business. My focus is set on the one person who can bust this case wide open. I strain my ears and idly suck at my chipped tooth, trying to pick out what I need to find.

Among the stupid, hateful, cacophonous sounds going on around me, I can hear a familiar voice. Amber, or should I say Racheal. She's in trouble. Two floors above me. Not trusting the elevator, I start running up the stairs, the graffiti and the down-and-outs flashing past me as I scale the steps two at a time. I don't even care how my knees are grating right now. My vision and thoughts have turned a deep, livid red. The sound of smacks and thuds are getting louder as I approach.

Why am I saving this gazelle, anyway? She lied to me. She might have put a lot of animals in danger... No, I just can't think like that. If she gets beaten to a pulp, or even... No... I can't have that on my conscience.

Finally, I reach the third floor, and the heart-breaking, horrible screaming is strongest here, alongside the thwacks and thumps that I'd heard down in the lobby. Number 312. The terror is deafening as I open the door. As I enter, the room is pretty spartan, to say the least. Not much more than a sofa and a bookshelf in this place, a moth-eaten mattress rolled up over a rusted-out bedstead, and a wiry billy-goat, wearing a tank-top, a pair of boxers that are more hole than fabric, and not much more to hide his dignity. He's holding a cracked, curled-up leather belt in his fist, towering over the gazelle at his feet, her cowering away from his blows.

"Racheal?" I say. A flutter of panicky recognition goes through her ears. The boyfriend is a little more physical in his reaction, though.

"Who are you, fuckwad?" He says, turning to me in that aggressive manner that goats have, particularly when you've invaded their space.

"Just want to talk to Amber," I say, but he tackles me before I can give any more details, and trust me, a tackle from those horns hurts. My bruised ribs buckle just a little bit more. He's on top of me. He's dropped the belt, but his fingers are now trying to wrap themselves around my throat. I resist, my own hands (even with one at limited function) struggling with his. I use my weight to throw him, lifting a shoulder to send him sprawling away. I stand, slowly, my back giving me trouble alongside my knees, but he's already picked up a straight razor from the nearby cabinet. He flourishes it, lashing out at me, the blade glinting eerily in the guttering light. He's trying to catch me off-guard, and though the blade cuts me once across the cheek, I charge headlong into him, the two of us crashing through the sofa, the razor skidding uselessly across the bare floor, along with my stunner.

Still, I don't need it. I start punching, in the general region of his face, and only with my good hand. I don't know why, but this feels satisfying, almost cathartic. A horrifying grin spreads across my face, showing nearly every one of my forty-two teeth, even the chipped ones. My flurry of strikes is short-lived, maybe only six or seven punches, as he finds a desperate strength within himself and bucks me off. I'm tumbling across the floor of the apartment again. Why the hell am I fighting this guy? What's his problem? In the split-second that I ponder these questions, he's dragged me to my feet. I can smell the desperation, and... what is that? This is unfamiliar...

I quash the thought, throwing him away and standing to ready myself for whatever he has up his sleeve or lack thereof. I've shoved him far enough away that there's a distance between us, but I'm steady on my feet, and so is he. Without thinking, he lowers his head and charges, trusting in his inborn ability to butt me to the ground again, but I dodge him much more gracefully than I'd expected. With the crunch of breaking plasterboard, his horns stick fast in the wall. He starts pulling and yanking at the wall, struggling there like you can't believe. Seizing the opportunity, I send a huge kick to his gut, and he slumps, clasping at his chest and stomach and whimpering, his horns still tying him down. I suppress the urge to kick him again. He's beaten. It's then that I really look closely at him and see the track-marks on his arms and thighs. He's an addict, and it's something nasty by the looks of things. That's what the unfamiliar smell was. He's probably more strung-out than a guitar.

I touch my fingers to the small cut on my face, and it stings. I'll need to get that looked at, but not right now. It isn't very deep, anyway. I calmly pick my stunner back up from the wreckage. The gazelle I'd formerly known as Amber has retreated to a corner to get away from the fight, trembling uncontrollably. Her eyes are streaming with tears, the welts and bruises already blooming under her fine fur. She's in shock, her mouth opening and closing mutely like a fish out of water. Her breathing is shallow and frantic. I don't have time to play nice-guy with her right now, but I need to know what's been going on. I crouch down in front of her, fixing her with a steely gaze. The gaze of a predator.

"Racheal," I say, and it snaps her immediately out of it. "Why did you lie to me?" She's clamming up after that question. I can already sense her natural flight reaction coming on, but I can't waste time here, and I'm still running on a well of furious adrenaline. I grab her by the shoulders and shake hard, turning us both so that I'm blocking the door.

"I just saved your life!" I scream at her, no longer giving a shit. "You told me Ayani Onyelé had gotten away from the fight. Every other animal was heading out the front doors, but you... No, you went out the back, just like Ayani. She had to have an accomplice! You! Just tell me I'm lying!"

A horrible silence forms a cloud around us, but I know I'm speaking the truth.

"You never mentioned exactly where she went," I say, reigning in my anger. "Faulty memory is one thing, but I'm damn sure you'd see where your zebra co-worker went. Zebras aren't common in Coldwater. I scented those pheromones and body oil out back of the bar. Your body oil. It was as plain as the day is long."

The goat that I left stuck in the wall gurgles something under his breath. I let go of the gazelle in my grip and stand up, crossing to his side, bending down to hear him better. Racheal (or Amber or whatever she's calling herself) sits petrified with fear.

"What was that?" I ask him, menacingly. "You've got to speak up, boy. I don't hear so well these days."

"Bastard…" he whispers, his breath wheezing and ragged. "You broke my fucking ribs…"

"Yeah, sure sounds like it," I say. "And if you want the remaining twenty or so to stay intact, you'd better start talking."

"Fuck you…" he rasps. I kick him again, square in the chest. I feel something give way under my foot, and he bleats in pain before he starts sobbing, still swearing incoherently and trying to threaten me as best he can.

"Nineteen left, loser," I say. "Want to try for one more?"

I pull my leg back, ready to boot him again, but before I can, Racheal has wrapped her arms around me in an attempt to stop the violence. Needless to say, it catches me off my guard.

"No! Don't hurt him anymore!" She screams. "I'll tell you everything… Just don't hurt him!"

I look into her bruised and battered face, dumbstruck. Unconsciously, my mouth falls open. Why is she protecting him? What on this green Earth can she see in this trash pile of an animal that's worth protecting? As soon as I realize how my face looks, all creased and stretched by rage, I snap my mouth shut, despite the pain from the lacerations I've sustained over the last few hours. She releases her grip softly, and I turn my gaze to her.

"All right," I say. "But talk fast, and no bullshit. What happened?"

She relinquishes her grip completely and sits down quietly on the wreckage of the couch, and I sit down just beside her. The boyfriend is still out of it, so we're both pretty safe, as far as I can see. I take the pack of smokes from my pocket and offer her one. She takes it, immediately putting it between her lips. I think she needs it, and I don't blame her. I click my lighter, and the flame springs up. The release of nicotine after such a huge ordeal lifts her, even though the cigarette is dangling from lips that are gradually puffing up into every color of the damn rainbow.

"I got Ayani out of the club," she says, her fingers still trembling as she teases the cigarette, wincing as it leaves her split lip. "Gill had us covered. He knew something was going down."

Shit, why am I always the last guy to hear this? I can guess that Gill is the crumpled over bag of bones and organs softly whimpering on the floor, his horns still stuck in the building's masonry.

"Why and how?" I ask. "And not necessarily in that order."

"The packs were looking for her," she says, frankly. "Something to do with her being nobility or something, I dunno."

"Not good enough," I snarl, rounding on her like a hunter. I don't have the tolerance for dancing around a Maypole right now. She immediately curls back into the sofa, her ears flattening against her head.

"Drugs!" She cries. "They were wanting to ship drugs!

From their poppy fields! Gill knew they'd need an easy out, and he knew Ayani was with the Zebra diplomats! He just wanted to keep her here until the Spinelli pack upped the offer the Donati pack had made! Then the Donati guys just came around and took her!"

I stand up, my knees grating again, though not as painful now because of the rush of adrenaline I'm still feeling. My eyes never leave the cowering gazelle on that busted couch. Time to bring out the big guns.

"You're coming with me, you two-faced, double-crossing slut," I say coldly, wrenching her wrist and leading her, struggling and kicking, out the door.

Once we're outside, I drop the tough-guy act and let go of her wrist. Rather than running, she looks at me in shocked bewilderment.

"What was that for, you asshole?" Racheal shouts. "You almost tore my arm off!"

"Sorry, kid," I reply, "but I needed your beau in there to think I was the business."

"No need to be such a dick about it!" She says, still cradling her arm where I grabbed on.

"That's my job," I reply. "Sorry you had to be on the receiving end."

A moment passes between us, and I can still feel all the aggression and hatefulness in the air. The apartments around us are still having their horrid spats, as though nothing had even happened only one floor up or down from them. The radios are still blaring their inane nonsense, the children are still getting scolded or worse, and the rutting is still as raw and primal as a dinosaur's feeding habits.

She still has the cigarette between her swollen lips, though, in all the confusion, her spark has gone out. I once again proffer my lighter flame, but given my rough handling, she's none too keen to accept it. I make the universal 'go ahead' signal, and she lights the now rather soggy smoke, drawing in a huge puff of breath. I spot the staircases on either side of us. One up, one down. I really hope she doesn't want me to chase her. Luckily for me, she has no such ideas.

"I know you were scared of that waste of life in there," I say. "But you can trust me."

"Can I?" she says, snarkily. "You want me to think you're a nice guy? You've treated me like shit since you first saw me."

I think back to when we met. I sit on the top stair leading down. The images tumble in my mind. I make my answer count. Home run.

"No," I say. "When we met, you were scared of something. I knew that. You were hurting, alone, afraid. Now I understand why. I know you kept things from me to protect yourself from something worse. I understand that, too."

I hear her damaged heels clack over beside me and her rump place down beside mine.

"You never wanted any of this," I continue. "You just wanted a way out. Well, kid... you've found one. You need to go to the PD."

The air around me shifts almost imperceptibly. She's wary of coppers, which is understandable given her associations with a drug trafficker and her line of work. I lay a hand on her knee, calmly, comfortingly. She doesn't flinch.

"Tell them everything you told me," I say, still not meeting her gaze. "Ask for... Detective Tilton. He'll know what to do."

Not that I can really trust that slimy pig but mentioning his name might get the wheels in motion. I think I'll make a call on him, too, once I get back home to re-arm. Tonight's going to be a hell of a night. Unexpectedly, her hand has covered mine, the one I placed on her knee, and her horns are ruffling the fur on the back of my neck. I can't help but place a kiss on her brow.

"You're safe now... Racheal..." I whisper.

"One a.m. Arden Shipping..." she whispers.

It's about half an hour later, and the blue and red lights are flashing from the black and whites. Gill, if that's really his name, is being trussed into a cop-car, crumbling plaster still clinging to his horns, coughing and hacking and struggling to breathe. Racheal and I watch from a safe distance. I've already thrown my coat over her, to block out the spring chill. I'm glad I called the boys in blue out here, if only to get that creep arraigned, though the superintendent didn't really know or like why I was hammering on his door needing to use the phone. Once I told him the situation, he agreed to help. I had time to get out of the building, Racheal in tow, and the super said he'd hold up the cops as long as possible. I normally wouldn't bend the rules like this, but I'm on a time limit.

Curious eyes peer out of curtained and boarded over windows at the lightshow below them. I turn to Racheal, a serious look in my eyes. She knows what the look means. The coppers haven't found us yet, and I'm not willing to give a statement right now, not with everything I need to do tonight.

"They're going to arraign him for a while, a couple of days at most," I say to her, matter-of-factly. "I suggest making yourself scarce, too. Go visit with your mom in the Pastures."

I try not to think about whatever is waiting for him in the sound-proofed interrogation rooms at the precinct, but the usual little shudder I feel whenever I do think of them is conspicuously absent this time. Maybe my nerves have finally fizzled out, and nothing really scares me anymore, or maybe I feel like that bastard deserves everything he gets. The jury is still out on that feeling. I light another cigarette and look at her.

"He'll get at least eighteen months in the Meadow for what he's done to you," I say. "Not to mention the drug charges. And a restraining order wouldn't be a bad idea, for your sake. As for me, I can legitimately claim self-defense. Play ball with the cops and tell the truth. I have stuff to do. They'll find me in due course. Send them my bill."

Taking my coat back and stubbing out the cigarette, I make a dash for it, anywhere I can't be seen, though my bruised ribs, smoker's lungs and grinding knees protest to such treatment. I barely even register Racheal's faint goodbye as I get myself to the nearest phone booth, more by luck than judgment. Once I cram my ass inside, I dig around in my coat pocket for the scrap of paper with Bill's phone number on it. I lift the receiver, deposit a quarter, and punch in the numbers.

As I hear the dial-tone, I know where I need to go. I'd questioned Racheal a little further while waiting for the police, and she told me what I needed to hear from her recollections of Gill's dealings. Easttown docks, Pier 12, the Arden Shipping Warehouse, one a.m. Conroy can't be in with the packs. Why would they be after his son? And in so blatant a place?

The other end picks up, and it's Betsy who answers with a weak "hello?" I muster a few scraps of charm amid heavy breathing and pain to ask for Bill, telling her who I am. Soon enough, she passes the receiver to him.

"Mr. Loolin?" He asks. "What's up?"

"Hey, Bill…" I say, still catching my breath. "I found out who was responsible for your brother's death… you said you'd help me if I needed you… want to help me catch 'em?"

A few moments go by, then Bill answers.

"Jus' say th' word, Mr. Loolin."

I outline a plan, depositing another quarter just to make sure Bill gets it, speaking slower, and going over the significant details a couple of times. He needs to come armed and meet me at the Easttown docks at 12.50 a.m., and to say goodbye to his mother and tell her he loves her. We're expecting trouble. He slowly agrees to the idea, a grim rumble in his voice indicating that he knows exactly what I mean. I hate to get the guy mixed up in all this — he might die — but I need all the muscle I can get, and he needs closure on his brother. If that means plugging a few packsters, so be it.

Once that's settled, I turn to my own affairs. I slide another quarter in the slot and dial Jerome. He'll be at home now rather than at the clinic. A few tense moments go by before the receiver picks up.

"Jerome?" I say.

"Yeah, whazzit Rex?" His voice replies, half-asleep.

"I need you to do something for me," I say, more seriously than I've ever been with him,

"What?" He replies, a sharpness of fear tinging his words. He can hear the flint-hard warning in my voice, and he knows I'm about to do something stupid.

"I need you to call the cops. Ad-Vice. Tell them there's something going down tonight at the Arden Warehouse on Pier 12 in Easttown. Don't call them until midnight, okay?"

"Rex, what are-?"

"Tell Mom and Dad, I love them," I say quickly before slamming the receiver back on its hook. Having done that, I slump helplessly against the inside of the booth, sliding down the glass and steel until I touch the floor. That was the hardest phone call I've ever had to make. This whole thing is bigger than me, than Ayani or Racheal, bigger than Danny Arden or Bill, or anything else. The existential weight of it seems to be crushing me like a ton of stone, but I must get back up and stand on my own two feet, like a real corgi. Like dad... and grandpa... I slowly rise, absently taking a cigarette from my pocket that I don't even need, and call Sid's cab company, slotting another quarter in the machine.

Gun, check. Stunner, check. Recorder, check. A couple of other bits and pieces if I need to break in... I slug back a shot of bourbon, trying to calm my nerves and the sense of growing dread. Less than a quarter of the forty left, not that it matters. I don't know what I'll find in that warehouse, but I know it'll get ugly sooner or later. I put another Band-Aid on my cheek where the goat cut me. The stinging sensation flares up and dies off just as quickly. Don't know how long it'll stick to my fur.

I cross to the record player, ruffle through my vinyl collection, and pick out a slow number. Mallard Avenue Blue by Clarence Mohl and his orchestra. Fitting. I don't often play this one, but I just can't find it in my heart to sell it or otherwise dispose of it. The last time it came out of its sleeve was when Jen ditched me to pursue the bright lights of Tinseltown. Sad memories seem to either follow or precede this album. Like I said, it's fitting. Time is growing short.

Once the familiar hiss of the needle hits the record, I listen to the first overture, put on my hat, grab my keys, and hit the streets once more. As much as I make a big deal of that tune, I'd rather not stick around to hear it through. I don't think Eduardo will mind. If he does, I'll kick his ass.

Another cab ride sees me to the Easttown docks, and I hoof it to Pier 12 and the Arden Shipping warehouse. It's here that the deal will go down. I check my watch. Just a few minutes 'til the hour. I check my load-out one more time. Stunner is good and charged up in case anyone decides to get too friendly. Gun… just a .38 service revolver with six shots. Luckily, I've got a pocketful more of them. Going to have to make every one of them count if it comes to that. I spark up what feels like the thousandth cigarette I've huffed tonight.

Then my ears pick up that distinctive, heavy tramp-tramp across the concrete. Bill's here. His looming shadow dwarfs me into blackness. He's looking a lot more prepared for bad news, too. Gone are the familiar checked shirt and worn jeans, now replaced by army fatigues and a long trench coat that makes mine look like it could fit on a glove-puppet. He's not screwing around, though I think he went a little overboard.

"Mr. Loolin?" He drawls, that same laconic style he's always had but edged with a grim resolve.

"Yeah," I say. "You ready to catch your brother's killers?"

He pulls a pump-action from the depths of his coat, the barrel glinting a dull, oily blue in what little light there is around us. Given how big he is, it looks like a pistol in his huge grasp. He wields it the same way, just idly handling it in one of his meaty fists. His eyes set upon me, hard as stone and just as rugged. He puts a hand on the pump and racks a shell.

"Let's go," he rumbles.

We make our way through an upstairs window. It was simple. A few quick lengths of packing tape (always come prepared) and a forceful blow gained us entry with little noise or shattered glass to worry about. I climb through the busted window first, followed by Bill, his heavy frame thumping beside me, louder than I'd care for, but obviously not loud enough to hear below us. I motion for Bill to keep quiet, and silhouetted in the moonlight, I see his horns nod to me. We have to take this very carefully. I can't hear any sounds from below, but I know there's someone down there waiting for the deal.

From what I can guess, we're in the manager's office, the impressive desk and filing cabinets reaffirming that idea. The door will be locked. I don't have a lockpick on me, and even the slightest noise could draw someone's attention. Bill creeps up beside me, much stealthier than I'd have given him credit for, and, with one huge fist, slams the doorknob and lock from its place. I tense, thinking Bill might have blown our cover. A few seconds pass, then a minute. Nothing. I breathe a sigh of relief. A few more seconds pass, and Bill and I push open the door.

We're on the upper floor, a gantry lining the outer edge of the warehouse. The steel floor might give us away if we make a wrong step. From below, I can hear a faint sobbing, stifled by something else, possibly a gag. I slip forward to the railing, trying to keep my shoes from giving me away, and peer down. Below, illuminated in a pool of light, sits a female zebra. She's tied to a chair, a rag cruelly stuffed into her mouth and bound behind her ears to keep her from screaming. I recognize her face immediately. That's Ayani. Her mane is dyed a bright pink, and it flops at the side of her head rather than sticking up like a brush, but that's definitely her.

Opposite from her, similarly trussed up, is a cat of a deep blue coloration, with big, yellow eyes. I don't know that guy, but given the way he carries himself, and by the quality of his attire, I'd like to bet five to one that he's a member of the Arden family. His captors don't seem to have treated him too kindly. One of his eyes is going a livid purple, and rivulets of blood are coursing their way from his busted nose. Despite the obvious beating he's been through, he doesn't make a sound, his eyes set, cold and stony. He's not expecting to get out of this alive.

Around them are a bunch of dogs in sharp suits, gats in hand. Dobermans, Rottweilers, Alsatians... tough bastards. They're watching out for something. The main warehouse door is barely visible in the gloom, but that's not where they're looking. There's a small side door that they're watching intently, alongside their prisoners. My breath quickens as the tiny portal cracks open, and a male zebra in a caftan and thick glasses steps through. The resemblance is striking. He's escorted by a couple more of the pack, sweating heavily. I can smell the fear and anxiety wafting up from him, even from this faraway vantage. They park the poor guy by his daughter, her eyes wide with terror and desperation as she fruitlessly tries to plead with him and her captors through the gag. He just nudges the glasses back on his face, fidgeting like he wants to run. Fat chance of that happening, with so many guns trained on him and his daughter.

Out of the shadows beneath me, a new face strides confidently into frame. This particular pan belongs to a bulldog in a long coat, draped casually over his shoulders so as to maximize the message that, in this situation, he's the one calling the shots. Probably one of the capos, but I can't be sure. His cologne almost blocks out everything else in the room, as far as the old sniffer is concerned. At least I can rely on the element of surprise again. I can't smell his goons, and they probably can't smell me.

His heels click ominously, the sounds echoing from the walls of this mostly empty warehouse. He stops in the pool of light between the two bound figures and turns imperiously towards Ayani's father. A fat cigar juts from between his jail-bar teeth, a billow of smoke emanating as he speaks.

"Jambo, Ambassador Onyelé," he growls with a condescending air. "Glad you could make it. I'm sorry the Arden Shipping company couldn't send a representative to this little meeting, but… heh… Conroy ain't exactly normal."

The heavies chuckle at their boss' wit, and I see the ambassador tense visibly. I bet his nerves are completely shot. I reach into my pocket and click on the portable recorder. Audible only to me, I hear the hiss of the tape. I don't want to miss anything after the usual pleasantries, and this'll be good evidence in court, should it come to that… if I get out of here alive. Ambassador Onyelé starts forward, stumbling, not in a threatening manner, but in a way that suggests he's a worm wriggling on a hook.

"Mister Loretti," he says, his accent piercing every word. "I have already given you many concessions. Why do you take my daughter?"

I start to work my way around the edges of the catwalk as quietly as I can.

"The concessions ain't good enough, Ambassador," the

bulldog (who I guess is Mr. Loretti) says, puffing out a huge cloud of cigar smoke. "You need to give us more."

I stop in my tracks, leaning over the railing to get a good ear, the recorder still hissing inaudibly. I even try to get it closer to what's being said. I look to Bill… and he's not there. I didn't even see him leave! If he goes charging in, he'll ruin the whole operation! There's a set of steel stairs near me. Do I go down and hope they don't hear me? Ugh… I need to keep focused on what's happening. Loretti speaks once again.

"Ambassador Onyelé, we need your official stamp of approval," he says, in a manner that's so oily I think I'll need another shower when — if — I get home. "You want to keep your daughters safe, isn't that right?"

I watch cautiously, halfway down the steps. His goons haven't heard me. I can see the backs of the two dogs guarding the stairway. The Ambassador thinks for a second, but I can see a fire in his eyes that I've only ever seen a few times before. Fight or flight. He's chosen to fight.

"Mr. Loretti…" he begins. "You can do what you want to me, but let my daughter go. Your dirty business is not mine! I refuse to move heroin for you anymore!"

A silence falls over the assembled animals like there's a thunderbolt ready to strike. Then it does.

"Okay," says Loretti, before casually drawing a revolver and shooting Ambassador Onyelé square between the eyes. The blood and brain matter splash across a wide area behind him, including his tied-up daughter. His lifeless carcass slumps helplessly to the floor. Ayani's muffled screams fill the empty space.

"There's always another Ambassador, right boys?" He smirks to his men. "Kill her and the cat, too. Do what you

208

want. The OPD won't be here for a while. And save the carcasses. They'll be worth something as meat for Don Donati's more… epicurean tastes."

The hench-dogs chuckle darkly in response, turning hungry eyes to the zebra and cat still tied up in their midst. I fumble for the revolver in my pocket, knowing this is already turning into a shit-show. Ayani screams again, the sound still muffled by the gag in her mouth, and Bill comes crashing out from some unknown angle, bellowing loud enough to wake the dead and blasting away with the shotgun he's been carrying. He must have found a secure way to the ground floor. Not even wondering how, I charge down the last few steps, the handle of the gun finding its way to my hand.

Before I even reach the bottom, it's a bloodbath, but I can't see hide or hair of Loretti amongst it all. But that's not the point. Ayani is closest to me, so, amongst the gunfire and the chaos, I crawl my way over to her and tip her chair, and she crashes down beside me. She's terrified, whimpering and murmuring through the rag stuffed in her mouth. Even through the cordite and blood, I know she's terrified from her smell. It was a wisp on the air I smelled long ago.

I untie her ropes and remove the gag. The grease and blood of her own father's brain is still staining her, but I can't let that get in the way. Before she can say anything, I motion for her to go and get out of here. She freezes up, another prey in the crosshairs… St. Roch, NO!

I tackle her to the ground behind a stack of crates, just as another hail of gunfire slices past us. She's as shaky as a political promise, but I drag her to her feet and shove. We're behind enough cover for it to be a safe move.

"GO! GO! GET OUT OF HERE!" I shout, and, almost

like the walking dead, she shuffles along to the back door that I only just noticed... that's where Bill came in. I look around. He's ducked behind some more crates, the occasional bullet flying past his ears, but none connecting. Keeping my head down, blind-firing a couple of rounds, I crouch-walk over to him, the hot lead filling the air until I finally get down beside him.

"I'm sorry, Bill!" I yell, but it doesn't seem to register. He stands back up, his bull-headedness taking over his common sense, and he unloads one last blast of his gun. Then one fatal crack sends a spray of blood over my face. The gaping hole in his chest tells me I'm too late.

Bill's head hits the floor, and for a flash of a second, those bovine features change to those of a greying bear, eyes bereft of life, lolling drunkenly around, the smoke and gunfire our only companions. The vision leaves as quickly as it came, and I duck my head down amongst the packing crates once again. Got to stay focused. I'm rattled but still determined and fighting for my life. *One of us made it through for a reason, Boscoe, if only to mourn the one lost.* I check the chambers on my old revolver: two shots before I need to reload. By St. Roch, I hope Tilton gets here soon. As much as I hate him, I can really use some backup!

Suddenly, the gunfire stops. A pregnant pause seeps over the area. I take the time to chamber a few more rounds. Then a mocking voice calls out.

"Hey, whoever you are back there, we'll find ya, and we'll fucking kill ya."

Shit... they're gonna be closing in on my position. I say a prayer to St. Roch, chamber my gun, think about Mom and Dad... Boscoe... Jen... then, out of the corner of my eye, a red and blue light starts flashing. I smell a fragrant undertone of panic. I would smile, but my beaten, bruised face can't manage it, and my beaten, bruised spirit isn't far behind. Soon enough, the sirens blare behind them. I stand and raise my hands, my gun dangling from my thumb in a gesture of subservience, and Marcus Tilton bursts in with his goon squad; the rookies who don't know him any better, and Vincent Bose, his personal lapdog (though I don't like using the term). Arrests are made, and soon enough the question of interrogation comes up, and I offer my paws freely.

"Okay, Llewellyn, whadda you know?" comes the whiskey- and cigar-tainted breath of Marcus Tilton, now sporting a lovely bright pink lump on his chin. Not the best interrogation technique, but my ravaged and bruised body would give anything to be away from here. The slate-grey walls around me do nothing for my mood, but if I can't humiliate this asshole publicly, I might as well do it privately.

"Okay, you want the skinny? Fine... Better have your toadies take notes...

"Ayani was mad at her old man because he wanted her to keep up the family name... you know, bring them out of the gutter. Nobility they may be, but it's a low nobility. That's why they all carry Spirit Keys... they still hold to their traditions. They couldn't let go of their roots."

I flourish the little sliver of wood in Tilton's face.

"It was torture for her, so she ran away, far from the choking collar of obedience. Found an easy job, one where her differences could build up the money she wanted... off her own back, not her father's."

I notice a few dogs amongst the officers passing the door,

wincing at the mention of the word 'collar'. Superstitious drivel. What matters is that I've got Tilton's attention.

"That made her an easy target. She's away from her family, vulnerable. The only people she has to rely on are her co-workers, and down in Coldwater, you don't trust anybody."

"Yeah," says Tilton sarcastically. "So, what does this have to do with Arden's kitten?"

"Unfortunately for Danny Arden, he was in the wrong place at the wrong time," I pause. "But you know these places, Marc. They're all under some sort of protection racket. There was some animal tracing Danny, and as soon as he saw the resemblance, that was the lynchpin. That's when Rocco and his goons showed up under the pretense of having a night out. It was a kidnapping attempt gone bad. They paid the price for it, along with Danny and his buddies.

"Anyway," I continue. "The Donati pack wanted to branch out into narcotics smuggling from their compounds in the Zebra Nation. They had the perfect in-road on both counts. Ayani to give them access to her dad's political connections and bypass customs. The Arden boy was to give them access to the means to transport the goods once they had them. Two kidnappings to make their point known and to assure the cooperation of both parties."

I can feel the adrenaline pumping in my veins, washing away the hurt, but also ushering me into sleep. No, not yet. A thought suddenly occurs to me... Orcowitz... That's why he ran, to cover up his double-cross... No... Yes... He was there... Wait... the note, and sea-salt...

"But don't you think there'd be some middle-man looking to make an easy amount of cash?" I ask. "Someone with near enough intimate access to one of the victims?"

A few days later and I'm back in my office, sipping at a fine Hornbeam bourbon, my arm in a sling, my face almost bound up like a mummy, given how many bandages and plasters there are on it. Jerome really wants me to take it easy, apparently. The soothing sounds of Aubrey Wilson's band wash over me from the record player as I look down on the near-empty street outside my window. There's some pangolin in a trench coat out there, some flasher, no doubt, waiting for someone to shock for his little kicks. To be honest, it's someone else's problem tonight. I've done my part for the next few months, though I put in a call to have it seen to.

I was right. It was Benny Orcowitz that was trading secrets between the Pack and anyone with a swift dollar. He even played double-agent for the Arden family. Least-ways, he'll be in the Meadow until the judge puts him on parole. Apparently, he cracked like a nut under the tender ministrations of Officer Bose, but, if I'm being honest, I think he'd have cracked under a feather. Stubborn or not, Orcowitz wasn't exactly a tough guy.

Ziva was happy for the return of her sister but also sorrowful for the loss of her father. She paid me in full, and I took it. She's just a client, after all. I didn't say what part I played, but Ayani turned her eye toward me, a hint of gratitude in that cold, distant exterior I'd expected. Maybe warmth? I don't know. Did she really hate her father that much? Or was it gratitude for saving her? Probably not a good idea to dwell on the subject. From what I've heard, they're both heading back to the Nation anyway to bury their father in the tradition of his ancestors.

As for the Arden boy (Cesar, I think his name was), he's

back home with a story to tell and maybe a minor wound or two. I'm not sure where this is going to lead. Might be nice to have a business big-shot owing you a favor, but I doubt my involvement will ever reach Conroy's ears. That's probably for the better.

With my good hand, I pick up the bottle of whiskey. Even though there's nothing drinkable in there anymore, I turn it over, watching the last dregs of liquor form their legs on the side of the glass. It's not much, but it gives me a little comfort about this case. And to think… legs like those were the starting point. Oldsburg isn't a place for the naïve or the gullible. It's a city, another beast unto itself, red in tooth and claw… and hungry for blood.

I know I owe Tony Henderson a steak dinner tonight, but I have someone I need to see first. The music swells, and I have to go. I need to see a certain Betsy and tell her why her last son isn't coming home this Saturday. The guilty money burns against my paws all the way there… I've got a funeral to contribute to…

And I hate it when dames cry…